THE GOOD SISTER

Rachael Stewart

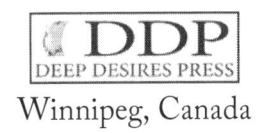

DDP
DEEP DESIRES PRESS
Winnipeg, Canada

Copyright © 2018 by Rachael Stewart
Cover design copyright © 2018 by Story Perfect Dreamscape

All characters are age 18 and over.

This is a work of fiction. Names, characters, business, places, events, and incidents are either products of the author's imagination or used in a fictitious manner. Any resemblances to actual persons, living or dead, or actual events is purely coincidental.

Visit http://www.deepdesirespress.com for more scorching hot erotica and erotic romance.

WIN FREE BOOKS!

Subscribe to our email newsletter to get notified of all our hot new releases, sales, and giveaways! Visit deepdesirespress.com/newsletter to sign up today!

For my very own Good Sisters, Louise and Rachael,

Thank you for being you, for kicking me
up the arse whenever I need it,
and for reading all the words!

ILYTTMAB,
Rxx

THE

GOOD

SISTER

CHAPTER ONE

ISLA SUNK DEEPER INTO THE hotel-grade sheets, reveling in the unfamiliar luxury and doing her utmost to block out the sounds of the waking world outside. She wasn't ready to join it. Not yet. Jet lag was new on her and it sucked.

Three days into her three-week mercy dash across the Atlantic and not only had she failed to leave her sister's home, she hadn't been able to deal with any of the paperwork that had traveled with her. The mere thought of it made her feel sick and she groaned, flinging her body out.

"Hey, baby, chill."

"What the f—" The words died on her lips, her startled blue eyes flying open.

At the opposite side of the bed, encased in the same bed sheet, was a man. A man that sure as hell hadn't been there when she'd crawled in eight hours prior!

The stranger blinked at her, his sleep-filled gaze trying to gain focus as a lazy grin broke across his features.

The air rushed from her lungs.

She'd know that grin anywhere.

It had filled her walls as a teenager, been stuck on the inside of her school locker, taped across her pencil tin, plastered inside her diary...

"Babe, you need to breathe, you're going blue."

She gulped.

He combed his hand through his trademark brown hair, pulling it out of his eyes. Piercing blue eyes that were now very much awake and studying her intently. "Sorry to startle you."

"Startle me?" she squeaked, grappling with the bed sheets to pull them closer to her chest, her heart racing.

She really needed to do something. To scream, move, get her naked body out of there. Anything!

"It was so late when I got back," he yawned, and she watched in star-struck fascination as he stretched his body out before her, his feet pulling the bed sheet to his waist. Her eyes widening with every inch of freshly exposed torso. Her gaze navigating across the subtle spread of dark hair over his pecs and the trail it formed down his abdomen, thickening just as it met with the edge of the bed sheet and disappearing beneath.

She gulped again. And again.

She had never been this close to a naked man in all her adult years and one on this par had her unacquainted-self in a spin. He had the tanned and toned physique of an airbrushed, artificially processed pin-up. Only he was most definitely real and only an arm's reach away.

"You were dead to the world," he shrugged, his muscles dancing hypnotically with the move, "I didn't have the heart to wake you."

He delivered the words so casually, their meaning clearly explanation enough for him. But for her...Isla scanned her memory banks, desperate for any reason as to why this man, *of all men*, would be here. With *her*.

No, correction, not with her. With her sister!

And there it was. The reason. Her twin.

It always came down to her. It should have been enough to spur her into action, but it didn't. Immobilized in sheer disbelief, her eyes raked over his features, ardently comparing the man before her and the man from the screen. It couldn't be him. It just *couldn't*.

He was the same, and yet age had given him an edge. Or maybe it was the five o'clock shadow tarnishing his boy-like charm? His square jawline brandished Devil-may-care stubble that accentuated his sculpted, full lips. Lips that she'd once stared at for hours on end, even pressed her own to, while her mind conjured up all sorts of fantastical scenarios. They had enthralled her then, but in the flesh…she couldn't tear her eyes away.

Not even her state of shock could dispel the mounting excitement within her. Or the acknowledgement that the man before her was even more attractive…more enthralling…more enigmatic in real life.

"Of course, now that you're awake"—her eyes flicked to his as he spoke and she was pinned by the sudden heat she saw there, fear sparking with the unwarranted excitement—"there's no reason for me to be so kind, is there?"

As rhetorical as his question was, her brain was screaming there was every reason. She knew she had to take action, but her body wouldn't listen.

He advanced toward her and the bed dipped with the shift in weight, titling her inward as she went with it.

Do something! her panicked subconscious screamed at her. *This won't end well!*

He was now close enough to smell, the faint hint of cologne invading her senses, drugging her with its heady masculine scent. He lowered his face to hers, his hair falling forward to brush against her cheek as she instinctively proffered her lips to his.

Just one little kiss, she told herself, her eyelids fluttering shut, *I owe my teenage-self that.*

He lifted the covers to reach around her and an air-conditioned draft invaded the bed clothes, sweeping across her already sensitized front and startling her nonsensical brain.

"Wait!" she blurted, tugging the sheet back up before his lips hit home.

He froze, his eyebrows raised in question, his strong and perfect nose just millimeters above her own. *What are you doing? This is the stuff of dreams, your dreams!* She looked to his parted mouth, his perfectly formed, utterly kissable mouth…

"Carrie?"

It took several seconds for Isla to register her sister's name, to let his usage of it sink in and take on board its meaning. *This mouth isn't yours to enjoy…*

"What is it?" he asked, his hand curving softly around her naked hip and sending treacherous sparks of delight ripping through her.

Helplessly, she kicked out, thrusting her body back in a desperate attempt to get away while she still could. But she couldn't have misjudged the ferocity of the move more as she found herself rolling uncontrollably backward, her body entangled in the bed sheets as she sent herself plummeting in an undignified heap to the floor.

"Christ!" The expletive came from overhead and she cringed at its pained intonation.

Gripping the edge of the bed, she pulled herself to her knees and peered over.

Mortification hit her full force as she took in his hunched and now sheet-less frame, his hands concealing his modesty as he gripped defensively at his manhood, making clear that she wasn't the only one to suffer from her poor maneuver.

She must have struck him, just *there!*

"Oh, jeez!" She scraped her hair out of her face. "I'm so sorry."

He squinted at her, and she ducked back behind the bed. Her breathing now coming in panic-filled pants. She was so far out of her comfort zone. A naked stranger was enough to make anyone hyperventilate, but when that stranger was the person of their dreams, it was something else.

"I can think of better ways to apologize," he said eventually, his voice husky with passing discomfort. "You going to come back and make it better?"

She purposefully tried to ignore him, and the answering call of her body as it toyed with a multitude of remedies, each more pleasurable and wondrous and damn wrong on so many levels.

Taking a steadying breath, she pulled the covers tight around her betraying buzz of a body. She needed to focus and get the hell out of there.

Scanning the floor, she frantically hunted out the briefs she had tossed aside the night before. The place was an utter bomb site, three days and she'd already transformed her sister's pristine haven into a state of chaos. Carrie would have a fit if she could see it now.

That's if she was still alive after Isla had finished with her. "Just be me for three weeks," her sister had pleaded, "it's not like your life can't wait for you."

Well, I tell you what, sis! she internally berated. *It was already a mess enough without this blasted complication adding to the mix.*

"You need a hand down there?"

How about both hands, right now, her mutinous body begged as her mind wrestled for control and demanded he stop speaking entirely. Just the sound of his all-too-familiar baritone sent her heart on a crazy dance.

Pushing to block him out, she grappled with the protective cover of the sheet and crawled to the end of the bed, disturbing piles of discarded bank statements and documents as she went. Those knickers were definitely here somewhere!

Why couldn't her sister have at least warned her? How could she be expected to successfully become her when she'd left out such a pertinent fact about her personal life? She was going to kill her. But first she needed that damn underwear!

"You looking for these?"

Oh no!

Begrudgingly, she raised herself onto her knees, gripping the sheet right up to her neck as she forced herself to face him once more. And promptly combusted.

He was on his side, casual as you like, one leg bent to rest his arm across it as he dangled her evasive briefs in front of him.

Her mouth went dry, her jaw dropping as she helplessly devoured every perfectly toned muscle, right down to his already stiffening manhood. No ill aftereffects there, evidently. She swallowed hard, he would have coaxed a moan from a nun!

"It's all still there, I assure you."

Her eyes flew back to his, heat soaring in her cheeks as he spied her focus.

"It's only been a couple of weeks and yet"—he gave her a bemused frown—"the way you're looking at me, it's like you've never seen me naked before."

"You could say that," she blurted, moving to snatch the briefs from his grasp and collapsing back to the floor.

She wasted no time shimmying them on, the sanctity of the bathroom was only seconds away, and careful to keep her back to him, she shot to her feet.

"I need the bathroom and you need this." Blindly, she tossed the bed sheet at him, a desperate attempt to get his god-like body covered up as she made a beeline for the bathroom door.

He chuckled after her and she risked a backward glance, taking in his amused state as he made no attempt to cover himself...*not even a little!* She swallowed as her sights locked south. *Fuck, he's beautiful.*

"Loving the undies, babe"—her eyes snapped to his and he gave a devilish wink—"never took you as the kind."

What the hell? She looked down to where his gaze rested on her arse and her cheeks flushed anew. *No. No. No.*

They were her novelty briefs, found in a department store's bargain bucket. One cheek christened with a bright pink handprint and the other had "Spank Me" splayed across it.

Could this get any worse?

She raced into the bathroom and almost yelped as her alien blonde-haired reflection greeted her—*it's just you, you idiot!* A week and the color switch from red to honey-blonde still irked her, but it had been necessary. A bonkers move, but necessary thanks to her sister's bleached appearance.

Maybe getting off with her sister's male companion could prove to be just another bonkers but necessary move?

Shut the fuck up, Isla!

She kicked the door shut and pinned her back to it. Fear that he would try and follow both exciting and petrifying her as she told herself not to permit him entry on any grounds. Despite the quiet of the room, her ears rang with her out-of-control heartbeat and she didn't need to look to know her nipples were taut with blatant arousal.

This couldn't be happening to her. She prided herself on her unwavering control where the opposite sex was concerned. She never let that complication enter her life. She'd seen enough mindless passion and so-called love turn twisted and ugly to last a lifetime, and with adulthood had come a barrier that no man had threatened. Until now.

But then, this man wasn't just anyone to her, and Carrie would have known that. It was upsetting that she had kept such a huge thing secret. And from her, of all people.

Or there was another possibility—perhaps Isla was simply losing it? Perhaps the emotional turmoil of watching her business, the joy of her life for the past ten years, fold beneath her, had had an even more severe effect on her mental health than she had first envisaged. And now, her subconscious was conjuring up the fantasy of her youth in some sick and twisted coping strategy.

It was a reasonable possibility…wasn't it?

She pushed the door ajar just enough to set her eyes on the tanned Adonis now sitting at the edge of the bed, his head bent forward as he scanned his phone.

Reasonable, but absolutely, categorically, may-the-Devil-take-me-now, not the case.

It was him, and every element of her being knew it.

Bradley King, star of the sitcom "Our Life", the series that had achieved global fame and took its stars to the level normally reserved for movie A-listers alone. He spent his time on the other side of the camera now directing and running his own production company, but with a look like his, his change in career was a goddamn crime.

Her mouth watered as her eyes drank him in and a strangled sound invaded her ears.

Immediately, he glanced up, his eyes locking inquisitively with her own and she realized with horror that the sound had come from her own throat.

Swiftly, she slammed the door, but not before his husky laugh reached her burning ears.

What in blazes had gotten into her? And him, for that matter?

He was right, it had only been two weeks, but the sight of her behind in those tight-fitting and ridiculously out-of-character briefs had his cock positively jumping.

How had he not noticed how perfectly full her derriere was until now, or how appealing the curves of her hips were when she walked?

Beautiful women were hardly scarce in his line of work, but this one, right now, had him behaving like a hormone-fuelled teenager. He was having to exercise every bit of control to fight the urge to drag her back to bed.

For his sanity, maybe phone sex was something they should consider going forward. Two weeks was clearly too long to go without a fix.

Staring long and hard at his phone, he tried to concentrate on his emails, scanning for anything that looked urgent, but all he could see was "Spank Me" adorning one deliciously curved cheek.

"Babe…you coming out of there?"

Even he could hear the choked desire in his voice. He needed to have her. It was no use trying to do anything remotely work-like until he had. It wasn't really a surprise when he'd spent the last ten days filming on Santorini with bikini-clad women trying to coax him away with every service under the sun. Not that any of them could compare to the one currently squirrelled away in the bathroom and behaving like some…well, some nut job!

He frowned, his thoughts turning to the last time they had been together and the events that had then unfolded. Maybe he really had gone too far, if two weeks wasn't enough to get her back to her old self…

Out of the corner of his eye, he saw the handle to the bathroom door shift and he shot to his feet, ready to stride across the room and make her forget any possible misgivings. But as she stepped out, he stopped dead. "Are you feeling okay?"

Her cheeks were streaked a feverish pink, yet the rest of her remained uncharacteristically pale. He couldn't make out if it was the lack of her customary tan that had him concerned or if she was actually sick. Her creamy skin almost blended into the ivory satin gown she now wore tight around her body, the delicate fabric doing nothing to assist his wavering control as it clung against her salacious curves, flaunting the two hard peaks mercilessly beckoning him. Sick or not, her body was giving him other messages that he was all too ready to respond to.

For Christ's sake, get your head out of your pants, King!

The least he could do was ascertain her wellbeing first.

Dragging his eyes back to her face, he watched her mouth fall open as if to speak but then she promptly closed it again, her vivid eyes flashing wildly.

What the hell's going on?

He stepped toward her and to his surprise, she took a step back, her arms moving to take up a protective hold around her waist, her obvious discomfort halting him in his tracks.

"What is it?" he probed, suddenly unsure he wanted to hear her answer but needing it all the same.

"Br-Bradley..."

She stumbled over his name, dropping the abbreviated "Brad" she always used. That in itself spoke volumes, if he chose to dwell on it, which he wasn't about to.

"You feeling okay?" he asked again, his fingers thrusting through his hair as he pushed back the foreign unease spreading through his gut. This wasn't about him. It couldn't be.

She shook her head, the move sending a quiver through her free-flowing hair that he rarely saw unadorned with a styling accessory or product of some sort.

"I'm a little under the weather," she conceded quietly, her accent taking an unidentified turn and pricking his unease, eradicating any sense of relief that she hadn't told him outright he was the cause of her distress.

He raised a casual hand to the doorway, "Perhaps some breakfast will make you feel better, I can rustle us up—"

"I'm not hungry," she cut in, her eyes now fixed on a point somewhere behind him, her body unmoving in the bathroom doorway.

"Then why don't you come back to bed?" he pushed, looking to the crumpled haven that he'd been so desperate to pull her back to. Right now, he'd settle for some simple spooning if it meant she would lift this weird persona that he had no idea what to do with.

"I think you should go."

What?

A chill ran down his spine. There it was. The confirmation he hadn't wanted. This wasn't about being ill, this was about them. It was about him.

Idiot!

He shouldn't have turned up without testing the ground first. At least if he'd spoken to her, he could have saved them the embarrassment of this face-to-face encounter.

"I hope it wasn't the shock of finding me here," he said, his fingers returning to his hair as he tried to give her a sheepish smile, one that he hoped would ease the situation. He wasn't always an arrogant ass. He could be soft if that was what she needed. "I really should have told Lara to check with you first."

"Lara?" she frowned, her eyes still working hard to look anywhere but at him.

Did she really find his presence so off-putting?

Suddenly the fact that he stood entirely naked before her, bothered him. He felt exposed both inside and out. Striding across the room, he made for the chair on which he'd deposited his clothes the night before. It was about the only surface not cluttered with "stuff" in the normally immaculate room.

"Yes, I told her to message ahead to say I was coming," he started to explain while picking up his jeans and thrusting his legs into them, grateful for the minor distraction. "I should have asked her to check you were okay with it."

"Oh," she nodded, her eyes had followed him but her body remained fixed in the bathroom doorway making it ever more clear that she wished to be anywhere but near him.

Christ! Two weeks and she can't even stand the sight of me. Well, fuck this.

"Look, I'll clear out and give you some space." He grabbed up his shirt and shrugged it on, his fingers starting to make swift work of the buttons. "I thought two weeks would have been plenty of space for you, clearly I was mistaken."

Promptly, she came alive, hurrying across the room to close the distance between them. "Bradley, I'm sorry"—she reached her hands out to halt his own over his shirt—"it's not you."

It's me, he mentally finished for her, refusing to let in the bitter tide of rejection. There were other women out there, plenty that would more than happily take her place, even if they didn't possess the same appeal.

He waited for her to continue, but she was quiet, her eyes fixed on where her hands rested upon his. Her touch so light that he could feel her fingers trembling. She really was far from alright…

"Then what is it?" His voice turned soft, his concern for her wellbeing overriding. He freed one hand to gently cup her face, coaxing her to look at him, to be honest with him.

She raised her lashes slowly, her eyes widening with such sincerity that he was struck by how innocently beautiful she was. Stripped of the tan he was so accustomed to, she had a porcelain complexion that he found fragile and strangely appealing.

"I really am out of sorts," she whispered, the deepness of those big blue orbs holding him captive.

The possibility that he might have misjudged the situation kicked him in the ass, his stomach twisting over his arrogance. He'd been so caught up in it not being down to him that he hadn't considered she could genuinely be ill.

"I'm sorry you're not feeling great." He gave her a small smile. "But I have to say I'm relieved."

"You are?" Her soft breath brushed over the exposed V of his chest and his body came alive over their new proximity.

"After how we left things?" He raised his brow, his thumb dipping into the groove between her chin and lower lip, stroking back and fore as he held her eye. "Absolutely. I'd hate to think that was the cause of this."

She wet her lips—*is it nerves that drive her tongue, or is she feeling the same magnetic pull now that we're so close?* "No, it's not you."

"Phew," he breathed, his keen eye taking in the rising flush to her skin, the way her eyes were dilating, her lips glistening…

"I just don't want you to catch it," she rasped, her words delivered seemingly on auto-pilot but reminding him all the same of her illness.

"You're worth the risk," he said. "Let me look after you?"

Her eyes dropped to his mouth, the move all-the-more telling, but she said nothing.

"Why don't I get us some breakfast?" he suggested, although food was the last thing he craved. "It might make you feel better."

She gave a small shake of her head, her eyes still on his mouth, turning almost fearful. "I think I just need to rest."

"There must be something that you fancy?" he persisted, his lips throbbing with the sudden urge to kiss the right response out of her.

He watched her swallow, hard, her tongue dragging over her bottom lip. *She fancies something all right…*

"How about it?" he asked, not even sure himself to what he referred. Food or sex? He knew which had his vote.

She peeped up at him, and their gazes locked, the fierce heat of desire soaring between them.

Hot on the tail of feeling shunned, he was past being gentlemanly. With more force than he intended, he crushed her against him and as her lips gave way to a startled gasp, he used the opportunity to stake his claim, his mouth working over hers with almost punishing intent.

God, she tasted sweet. Even sweeter than he remembered. Her deliciously tentative mouth coming around to the invasive pressure of his as he stoked her into a fire that married his own. And then it was impossible to work out who was the driver as her fingers forked aggressively through his hair, her head tilting to permit him the access he craved, his tongue toying raptly with hers as her throat gave way to little sounds that had his entire being craving more. He wanted her screaming his name, her body crashing with the force of the orgasm he knew he could give her.

Moving swiftly, he cupped her thighs through the satin and lifted her, parting her legs around him as he did so and walking her to the bed, not once breaking his assault on her mouth, not that he could have, her hands had his head well and truly pinned. And not that he was complaining either. She was as hungry as he, and his pulsating cock was lapping it up as it pressed against the hard fabric of his jeans, desperate to be free.

All in good time…first, he wanted her good and ready.

Lowering her to her feet once more, he traced his fingers up the sleeves of her gown, pausing at the edge of the robe and slipping his fingers beneath, loving the feel of her soft, warm skin beneath his touch and the whimpers he was coaxing from her lips.

The flimsy fabric put up no resistance as he slipped it from her shoulders, its downward fall enough to force the knot at the waist to come undone and taking the entire thing to the floor, leaving her full, round breasts bare to his wandering eye as he tore his mouth away and leaned back to drink her in.

He'd swear she was curvier and yet more toned. Where there once was bone, there was now a softness that his eyes and fingers couldn't get enough of. He wasn't fool enough to comment on her gain in weight, he had ribbed her enough about her lack of it in the past. The change couldn't have been more unexpected or downright cock-inspiring.

Even her breasts were bigger, their weighty mass filling his palms with flesh to spare. With awestruck fascination he moved over them, weighing them in his hands and rolling his thumbs over her sweet, rose-tinted nubs.

"God, yes!" she sighed, her head lolling back as she gave herself up to the pleasure, her heated reaction going straight to his groin, his own mouth parting in wonder as he found himself drowning in the sight and sound of her.

"Oh, don't stop," she gasped, her eyes heavy as she watched him.

"Don't worry, baby, I ain't going anywhere," he assured her, but as he said it, he let his hands drift to her waist. "I do want you to turn around though, so I can see your sweet behind in those glorious undies again."

She whimpered her response, her slitted eyes clearly struggling for focus.

"Turn, baby," he urged, using his palms to guide her. She went willingly, stopping when her back pressed up against his chest and, for a moment, he enjoyed the feel of her there, his cock pressed between the cheeks of her ass, her breasts thrust upward to the reunited caress of his hands, her head resting in the crook of his neck and shoulder. The sound and proximity of her panting mouth driving him to the edge.

"Bend over."

He felt her tense at his command and he trailed his fingers down either side of her body, his voice softening as he added, "Please, I need to see your gorgeous behind in those briefs once more…"

Slowly, she moved, bending one knee upon the bed and then the other. She now rested before him on all fours, her head raised to the wall ahead, her curvaceous behind and its taunting message filling his vision and sending him to hell.

"Good girl," he said, his voice laced with awe as he brought one hand up to splay it across her backside, mimicking the handprint beneath, taking pleasure in the feel of the ample flesh curving into his palm. She truly was beautiful and having her bent before him, so vulnerably exposed, left him humbled and burning with a barely contained need of his own.

She wriggled her hips beneath his stroke, her ass telling him that she was a more than willing participant to anything he had in mind. He rewarded her with a circling caress that made her whimper and rock.

Lifting his palm away, he watched in fascination as she pushed herself back toward him, her bottom beckoning for his touch again, the sounds escaping her lips coming from deep within and sending him dizzy with their erotic intonation.

"Don't stop," she whispered, her voice so low he only just caught it.

"What is it, baby?" he goaded. "You want this?" he cupped her ass once more with his palm, his hand moving rhythmically over her with increasing urgency.

She writhed beneath him in answer, her fists clenching and unclenching in the bed sheets before them.

He knew what she wanted, and he wanted to give it to her. They'd never gone down that route before, but there was no denying what was burning through their minds right then.

Using one hand to pin her lower back to the bed and forcing her behind to proffer up to him, he pulled the other back and brought it up hard against the curve of one cheek. The resounding crack timed perfectly with the cry from her lips.

He felt his cock weep with excitement and feared he would come there and then.

"Again," she cried beneath him and it was all he could do to carry out exactly what she asked, marveling at how her body bucked with each strike, the skin peeking out from beneath the trim of her briefs flushing pink as her moans became louder and ever more hardcore.

"Take them off," he commanded, his voice so hoarse he barely recognized it.

She wasted no time hooking her fingers into the waistband and shoving them to her knees. He did the rest, tugging them off and tossing them to the floor.

Mind now entirely lost, he thrust her legs apart, desperate to see how much she dripped for him.

He wasn't disappointed, the hairs surrounding her usually bare pussy, positively oozed with desire and he couldn't wait to dip inside.

Curving his hand over her crotch, he smoothed backward, slipping his fingers between her folds and relishing the dampened heat that engulfed them. She bucked as he made fleeting contact with her clit, a moan tearing from her throat and forcing a reciprocal groan of desire from his own.

"Spank me," she pleaded, the words breaking free on an anguished cry.

His fingers hovered over her swollen clit as he dared to ask, "Here?"

"Yes," she breathed.

Hell yeah, she doesn't need to ask twice!

Cupping his three fingers together, he spanked her clit, once, twice, and again. She lapped it up; every time he struck, she moaned, encouraging him to go harder, to give way to the raging desire threatening to consume him.

"More, more…" She was doing all she could to keep her ass thrust upward toward him, surrendering herself entirely to his attention and he took advantage of the position. Using his free hand to separate her folds, he exposed her entire nub to the spanking he was delivering. He was coming swiftly undone at the sight, sound, and feel of her, and there was nothing he could do to prevent it. Never before had she been this wanton, this brazen before him…

"God, yes, Bradley!" she cried, her hands fisting into the pillow ahead, her head thrashing this way and that as her thighs tensed beneath her. She was so close, he could see it in every muscle of her being, and fuck him if he wasn't about to come inside his jeans like some crazed youth. But did he give a shit? Hell no!

"That's it, baby, come for me," he ordered, his voice raw with need, his hand now alternating between slapping and rotating over her.

She exploded beneath him with earth-shattering intensity, her whole body convulsing wildly against the bed and the air turning blue with her profanity.

Not that he could judge as he collapsed against her, his own seed filling his pants in shameless abandon, his whole mind and body lost in the crazed heat of the moment.

There was no way in hell she would say no to him now. Not when he'd reminded her of how good their future together could be. But then why was she taking so long to give him her response? And why the weird behavior?

His mind trickled back to their last night together and how perfect it had been. Granted, it hadn't been as explosive as this, but it had been more than pleasant…

Right up until the moment he had said, "Will you marry me?"

CHAPTER TWO

WHAT THE FUCKETY-FUCK HAD SHE done? It was one thing to immerse oneself in some pornographic viewing and re-enact the scene upon yourself at the same time. Which, if Isla was completely honest, she had a tendency to do. After all, she may have sworn herself off the opposite sex and relationships entirely but that didn't mean she didn't respond to the same primal need that everyone else had. She was just very adept at getting herself off and enjoying a range of viewing materials and props while she was at it.

But to then give in to those base urges with a man that she had no right to even speak to, let alone share a bed with, was insane.

What was it she had said…spank me? SPANK ME!

Her cheeks flamed as she pressed her fingers against them, their cooling tips doing nothing to take away the edge.

And, Christ, if she wasn't about to throw her phone—*correction, Carrie's phone*—at the wall. The goddamn thing kept reciting her own welcome voicemail message over and over again, like everything in life was tip-top rosy and she wasn't about to descend into a whirlpool straight to Hell.

She'd been trying to reach her ever since she had awoken to an empty bed and a brief, but heat-inspiring note: *Sorry had to leave you, keep that pussy stoked for me, back later xxx*

She plummeted her hands into the sink, her hands cupping the ice cold water as she threw it over her face, her mind trying to quash the rush of emotion tearing through her. Was it shame, nerves, fear, excitement...all of the above?

And to top it all off, she'd actually had the gall to fall promptly asleep in his arms straight after, like it had been an entirely "normal" thing to do. Jet lag had a hand in that for sure, but still! One would expect to experience some disquiet after the deed to prevent falling asleep!

Was it possible she had become a heartless, sex-crazed sociopath? Or was she just so unhappy that she had lost sight of what mattered? Whatever the case, she wouldn't be able to think straight until she had spoken outright to her sister. Not that she had a clue what she was going to say. How exactly does one broach the subject? "Hey, sis, guess who I just shared an earth-shattering climax with? And here's a clue, he's your dirty little secret!"

"What a mess," she said to her reflection, her eyes disbelieving as they scanned her wet and too-flushed face. She reached out for the hand towel and rubbed it gruffly against her skin, marveling still at just how soft, fluffy, and fresh-scented it was. Her sister had all the finest things in life and that, as ever, included men.

Tossing the towel aside, she swept from the bathroom and cut that thought dead, unwilling to go there. She was past all that childhood resentment. She needed a man as much as one needed a gun to the head. They were a complication that she didn't have the time or inclination for.

Snatching up Carrie's phone from the side table, she dialed her again and after the same few rings, she was greeted once more by her own perfectly calm and professional recorded message.

She ended the call, staring at the phone screen as if it was in some way to blame for her sister's lack of response. What the hell could Carrie be doing that was so important she couldn't even answer the thing? They may have switched phones to maintain the charade but the damn thing would still be glued to her like a lifeline, holiday or not. And the thirty-or-so missed calls and crazy-lady voicemails Isla had left for the past three hours would all hint that this was actually a blasted emergency!

"Arghh!" she exploded, tossing the thing on the bed and jumping out of her skin as it started to ring on impact.

She snatched it up. "Carrie!"

"Isla?"

"Mum?" Confused, Isla rechecked the caller ID. "What are you doing with Carrie's—*my* phone?"

"She left it at home, darling. Is everything okay?"

"No!" That was a daft thing to say, she didn't want to worry the woman but she couldn't very well tell *her* what was going on! "I mean, yes, I just need to speak to her about…about a friend of hers. When will she be back?"

Silence.

"Mum?"

"I'm not sure, she didn't say."

Even through the phone, her mum sounded edgy, worrying Isla into asking, "Have you fallen out or something?"

"No, no, not at all," her mum blustered reassuringly. "It's lovely having her home. She's just the same, I worried Hollywood might have changed her, but…"

Isla smiled into the phone. "Mum, she was born for Hollywood, it didn't need to change her."

"Very true," she agreed, pausing momentarily before adding, "she really is so much like her father."

The last was said in such a way that Isla wasn't even sure she was supposed to hear it and to be frank, she wished she hadn't. The man had pulled their family apart, any reference to him was a curse in her book.

Pushing aside her feelings, she piped up, "So, come on, where's she hiding out? I've been trying to reach her for hours."

"She's out."

"Yes, I got that bit, Mum, but where?"

Again, silence.

She was about to prompt her when finally, she spoke. "She's out with Dan."

Ah, now her avoidance makes sense.

"Well, that's a good thing," Isla stated, shrugging off the mention of the guy, it made sense that he and Carrie would be out together. It would have been years since the two had seen each other properly. Besides, Dan was a big boy, he could look after himself.

"I just thought..."

"Mum, it's fine. Dan and I are business partners, nothing more."

"I know it's been a long time, honey, but I didn't want to bring back unwanted memories."

"Mum, I was a kid, do you honestly think I could have worked with him if I was still upset over his feelings for Carrie?"

"You didn't have to be the person stuck between you girls back then! It was a war zone and you were utterly miserable."

"We were hormonal and I was a besotted teenager, we all put it behind us long ago. Seriously, how old do you think I am?"

Her mum let out a nervous giggle. "Well, when you put it like that..."

"So, where are they? It's odd that she hasn't taken her phone."

"I really don't know where they are, she's keeping a low profile as you can imagine and enjoying not being tailed everywhere she goes, but it hasn't stopped her going out every day."

"She needs to be careful she doesn't blow it if she wants it to remain that way."

"I know, darling, and she is so grateful for everything you have done to go along with this charade. You should see how happy she is to be so free, as she calls it."

"I know, Mum, and I know she needed it. I couldn't really believe it when she asked, I never thought it possible that she would find the press too much, but…"

"I think there's more to it than that, honey."

"Like what?"

"I don't know, but I get the feeling something happened before she left. I've never seen her quite so unsettled."

"She's always unsettled, Mum."

"This time it's different. It's like she's running away."

Her mum was worrying unnecessarily, Isla was sure of it. "I'm certain she's fine, Mum, but I'll talk to her when I finally manage to get hold of her. Can you get her to call me when she gets in?"

"Sure, darling. Now, tell me, what have you been up to? I keep meaning to get out there and spend some time with your sister, but…well…LA isn't really my sort of scene."

What she really meant was, the risk of bumping into their father was too great. "You should do, Mum, it's fab, she's got a fantastic place, lovely pool and garden, an awesome entertainment system in every room…"

"But what of LA?"

"Erm…the airport looked good."

"Isla! Are you telling me you've not been out yet?"

Busted!

"No, not yet…but I will." The last thing she wanted to do was stress her mother out with her newly found agoraphobic tendency or have her mother embark on a lecture that would only be hypocritical. "I'm just taking my time, I've been so busy and stressed twenty-four-seven that I'm enjoying the chance to finally relax and not have to do anything."

"I get that, sweetie." She could hear the concern in her mother's voice and mentally slapped herself for actually making her worry more. "I must admit this past year, watching you work so hard, some days I just wanted to drag you home and lock you up until you got some sleep but you were so determined to make it all work."

Isla scoffed, her stomach twisting with self-loathing. "And look where it got me."

"Darling, it's not your fault, the odds were stacked against you. Personally, I couldn't be more proud of you."

"Proud. Are you crazy, Mum? The business belly-flopped."

"Not through any fault of yours, darling. These big corporations, they don't care who they trample on to achieve their goal."

"It was my club, Mum, no one else's. If it couldn't cope with some healthy competition then it wasn't worth saving."

"I thought Dan—"

"Dan tried to help and it wasn't enough." And she owed him, big time. He would have given her more, but she couldn't and wouldn't accept charity. She felt the failure like a physical blow.

"You need t—"

"Mum, can we talk about something else, I'm on holiday." She couldn't think about the business yet. She wasn't ready. She knew she had to at some point, but right this second she just wanted to pretend that part of her life wasn't happening.

"Sure, sweetie…"

She spent the next half hour catching up. It was easy to pass time with mum; they were so similar, if they hadn't been mother and daughter they could easily have been best friends.

When she'd finally said goodbye, her mood had relaxed somewhat. She would have been lying if the first mention of Dan hadn't kick-started a pain in her gut. They had all grown up together. The three of them inseparable. And as her feelings had changed for him, so too did his for her sister.

He wasn't the only boy that had become trapped under Carrie's spell either. Throughout their early teens, right up until the point she had left with their father at sixteen, Carrie had bewitched many a guy and Isla had been left to pick up the pieces. They all turned to her after they'd been rejected, like she was some runner-up prize, always second choice.

She had actually fallen for it once. Never again.

Dan hadn't stooped so low as to treat her like that and she loved him for it. She wasn't *in* love with him. Not anymore. She had accepted long ago that her feelings weren't reciprocated and had learned to be content with the role of best mate.

The only reason her mum's news still gnawed at her was worry for him and his own feelings for Carrie. It had taken him a long time to move past her when she had left and Isla was painfully aware of how he struggled to maintain any relationship for longer than a few months. Always looking for the next conquest, never fully satisfied. Carrie had left a huge hole in his life that he had yet to fill, and Isla had no doubt that Dan's feelings for her sister still burned beneath the surface. She just prayed her sister wasn't thoughtless enough to play with that fire. He didn't deserve to go through it all again.

But then, if this morning's events were anything to go by, she shouldn't need to be concerned about her sister and Dan. Not when her sister already had a man this side of the Atlantic. Something that Carrie hadn't so much as hinted at.

Now that did hurt. It really hurt.

Yes, she was mad that her sister's secrecy had led to a totally mortifying scenario that she should have been prepared for. Perhaps then she never would have ended up in the compromising position she was in now.

But it was more than that. It was the fact that Carrie had kept something this major all to herself.

Their weekly catch-ups were all about keeping each other up-to-speed with one another's lives, and that included the guys they were dating (or rather Carrie dated). So why hadn't she mentioned him, of all people? They had worshipped him as teenagers. She should have been chomping at the bit to tell her.

Or did she still see Isla as the weak and vulnerable younger sibling (by two minutes!) that would be traumatized by the news that her sister had yet again bagged the guy? God, how immature did she think she was?

She began to pace the house with newfound zeal. She needed to burn this off or she was going to go mad.

A run in the fresh air would do it. But then she wasn't permitted to do that, Carrie had expressly forbidden it. There were rules after all. Rules she *must* abide to. All of which, Carrie had compiled into a beautifully typed "Rules Sheet" that she had handed over as a parting gift.

As if Isla needed the added fuel to power her run, she thought she'd stoke her temper and reacquaint herself with the delightful list.

Stomping to the dresser—which looked more like a space-age entertainment zone with the huge rectangular TV mirror atop a stark white unit that she still hadn't fully fathomed to operate—she picked up the sheet.

"Just in case you should forget anything I have said..." her sister had smiled sweetly as she'd handed it over, as though it was a present or some other such nicety. Not a list of control-freak factoids that Isla was not allowed to deviate from.

Like she hadn't already done enough to convince people, she thought, glaring at her blonde reflection briefly before turning her attention back to the list.

Numero uno—the one that meant she couldn't take out her frustration by pounding the grounds of LA, stated:

> *1. Do NOT exercise in public. I know you love working out, but letting people see you sweat is disgusting and remember you are me. My home gym has everything you could possibly need and*

if not, get it delivered, my treat.

So exercising like a caged animal was a must. And as for the rest of the list…

2. ALWAYS wear makeup unless you're sleeping.

Or hanging out at home, Isla surreptitiously added.

3. Do NOT visit fast food joints. If you really need your kebab fix you can find it in a more suitable establishment where being papped won't be an issue! (But please remember you are a lady, a fork and knife were invented for a reason).

She actually laughed out loud at his one. Carrie had never eaten a true kebab if she felt cutlery was required.

4. Do NOT be seen inebriated.

Easy, Isla wasn't going "out-out".

5. ONLY wear clothing from my wardrobe.

A blessing in disguise! Nice clothing suitable for LA was a luxury Isla couldn't afford to buy before she came, so access to her sister's designer wardrobe appealed more than she cared to admit.

6. Please, please, please don't be caught wearing your god-awful glasses. You have contacts now. Use them!

Isla rubbed her eyes at the reminder, she was getting used to wearing the things but getting them in was another matter. Another rule she would add to the "only required when leaving the house" pile.

7. Try and be graceful, heels are a must for any social event.

This was easy. She wasn't planning on attending any social events, unless a trip to the supermarket counted.

8. Don't trust anyone to keep our secret, except Dad, everyone talks whether they mean to or not.

She cringed at the dad reference, and tossed the list aside, not wishing to look at the remainder as she knew it included him. She really had no interest in seeing him, let alone telling him what they were up to. And she supposed the "anyone" in Rule No. 8 covered Mr. Teenage-Fantasy himself.

What had her sister been thinking not to have told him? Did she not trust him? Did she not realize he was going to turn up and send Isla into a complete spin?

Perhaps if her sister had put as much effort into filling her in on her love life as she had into producing the "list", Isla could have at least behaved with some dignity that morning, rather than as a crazed buffoon. And also not succumbed to the wildly out-of-control desire that had all but consumed her and put her on autopilot to the most amazing orgasm of her life.

Well, it was entirely Carrie's fault when one looked at it that way!

Turning her attention to the minefield that was her sister's dressing room, she hunted out some gym gear.

Ten minutes later, her displeasure at the incarceration enforced by Rule No. 1 morphed into sheer relief as she held up Carrie's exercise "appropriate" attire—skimpy pink crop top meet short black hot pants. A public appearance in such an outfit was now far from her mind.

There must be something else. Something with a little more fabric. Tossing it onto the bed, she returned to the drawer and pulled out more of the same.

God, did her sister never have a "fat" day where she wanted something with a little more cover?

Ramming everything bar the set she'd extracted back in the drawer, she closed it and tried to calm her inner prude. It wasn't like anyone was going to see her after all.

Averting her gaze from every possible reflective surface, she changed into the outfit and legged it to the gym. The hamster run was just what she needed right now; it would be the perfect distraction to kill another hour and then she'd try to get hold of her ladyship again and confess all.

It had been four hours since Brad had left Carrie's house for his company HQ and not one of those had been spent productively. Not in his eyes anyway.

As soon as people got wind he was back, Lara was straight on him in his office with documents to sign, people to meet, places to go. In fact, he'd barely had five minutes in his own space and he was starting to feel claustrophobic.

Or was it his nagging doubts over Carrie's response to his proposition that had him pulling at his shirt collar?

"We can leave this lot until tomorrow, Mr. King."

Lara was looking at him expectantly, her eyes narrowed at him from across his desk.

She was probably trying to work out the true cause of his preoccupation. Her PA prowess would not be impressed if she knew that at that moment in time it was the memory of a bright pink handprint.

Or the fact that for the umpteenth time that day his mind was replaying the events of that morning. The very recollection of Carrie bent on all fours—

Lara cleared her throat.

Shit! Concentrate, King!

"Sorry, what was that?" he asked her, leaning forward in his chair, his hands moving to rest on either side of the paperwork Lara had deposited upon his desk minutes before.

What script was this again? He scanned the cover, but all he saw were black lines blurring into white, his eyes too tired to focus.

She gave him a surprisingly sympathetic smile. "I think you've had enough for today, you need to catch up on some sleep."

"Is it that obvious?"

She nodded, her blonde bob dancing. She pressed her glasses further up her petite nose and started collecting up the papers from the desk.

"I'm going to head out to Carrie's now." The words were out before he'd even processed the idea properly. He had always intended on going, but not until late evening.

Lara's hands stilled over the papers, her expression an unreadable mask. "Do you think that's wise? You would be better getting some rest."

Brad pretended not to notice the sudden edge to her voice. "No, it's fine, did you get those flowers I asked for?"

She straightened, one hand smoothing out her pencil skirt, the other clutching the papers to her chest as she raised her eyes to his, her professional exterior firmly reinstated. "Yes, Mr. King. I will just get them for you."

"Thank you, Lara."

She gave him a brief nod, turned, and fled. Not for the first time he wondered if he should have her transferred to another department, but in his experience it didn't matter who he got, the relationship always broke down eventually. Whether it was his perceived playboy image, concern for the women that came and went, or a form of jealousy, his personal assistants never lasted more than a few months.

Lara, however, was in her third year and although he didn't know the exact cause of her occasional slip in professionalism, she was an exceptional PA. So long as she did that well, the rest didn't matter.

Besides, he'd taken her on as a favor to his stepsister, Amy, and he wasn't about to go back on his word to her.

Amy had been in rehab with Lara and the two had emerged the best of friends. She had pleaded with him to give Lara a job, convinced that it was the only thing that would keep her on the straight and narrow. It had been an easy decision to make. Anything to have Amy happy and back to her normal self. If he could help another lost soul in the process, all the better.

The memory of those dark days haunted him and he pushed the thought aside. He didn't need to worry any more. Amy was doing great, she'd gone back to school and her studies were progressing well. As for Lara, she had turned out to be the perfect PA candidate. All was good. Now he just needed to focus on Carrie and where her head was at.

Before he had left for Santorini, he had believed there to be an understanding between them, a shared vision for the future. Now he wasn't so sure.

He pulled at his shirt collar once again. Lack of confidence didn't sit well with him, but he wasn't about to avoid the situation. He needed to have it out with her and get this dealt with. First, he would check she had recovered from whatever ailed her. And then he would raise the question once more.

As if on cue, Lara knocked and entered, a bouquet the width of the doorway in her arms. He knew he'd asked for something impressive but he still had to drive with the bloody thing on the passenger seat of his Lamborghini Aventador.

"I told you I can arrange to have it delivered." Lara said, picking up on his train of thought.

"No, I will do it."

"Are you sure? I'm just worried it's too big for your car, I could always take it on my way home," she persisted, smiling sweetly. "I would have got a smaller arrangement, but you insisted it had to be big and special."

"I sure did," he agreed, standing and walking around the desk to take the monstrosity from her outstretched hands. Who in their right mind would create a bouquet this unwieldy? "It's perfect."

Lamborghini or not, he would make the thing fit.

He was ramming it into the passenger seat ten minutes later when his phone rang. He scanned the caller ID, and ignored it. Continuing to shove the flowers down into the footwell, he caught his finger on a stray thorn and cursed. He thought they were supposed to take the damn things off to avoid such mishaps. They'd cost enough!

His phone kicked off again. Same caller. What the hell could she want?

Against his better judgment, he flicked to accept the call, putting it in the crook of his neck while he adjusted the flowers to prevent any beheadings as he lowered the door.

"What is it, Marie?" he snapped, really not in the mood.

"Well, seriously, Bradley, is that any way to talk to your mother?"

He took a deep breath, forcing down the words he'd been about to deliver as he made his way around the car to the driver's side. "I'm in a rush, can you tell me what you want so we can get this over with?"

"Why is it you always think I'm after something?"

"Do you really want me to answer that?"

"It's Amy."

He stopped mid-stride, his heart skipping a beat. "What is it? Is she okay?"

"It would be so nice if you actually showed me the same level of concern some—"

"Is Amy okay?" he spoke over her, he had no care for his mother's jealous ramblings right now.

"I'm just saying—"

"Mother!" he warned, his legs back in motion now as he scanned the busy parking lot and had no wish for anyone to overhear where their conversation was heading.

"Oh, she's fine, darling, for goodness sake."

Relief flooded him as he yanked open his car door and dropped inside, his head pressing back against the headrest as he slammed the door shut and let go of another deep breath. *Don't let her get to you.* "So, what is it?"

"I just learned that you are back in LA, which, by the way, is something one should learn via their son directly and not through the gossip columns."

He gritted his teeth against her condescending tone, his free hand reaching automatically for the steering wheel and clutching it tight. "I flew in last night, my own brain barely knows I've landed. I hardly expected it to be in the general domain already."

"You should know better than that, Bradley," his mother chastised, the way she purred over his name sending his knuckles white. "Anything worth knowing is readily in circulation, your whereabouts are no exception."

For fuck's sake! "What has my return got to do with Amy?"

"Well, you must know it's her birthday next week."

He took yet another breath. It had slipped his mind, but Lara would have reminded him. She would no doubt have a present ready and waiting.

"And?" he ground out.

"I've arranged a party for her, it's on Friday."

"You've done *what*?" It was partying that had got Amy into a mess in the first place. And although she had long been on the straight and narrow, she was terrified of a relapse, they all were. Save for their mother, clearly.

"Oh, come on, Bradley, calm down, the girl is going to be twenty-one."

"A party is the last thing she needs." *Which you would know if you actually behaved like a mother*, he silently added.

"I'm not going to argue with you." There was a hardness to her voice now. "This wasn't me ringing to ask permission to throw a party for *my* daughter. I simply wanted to say that as you are back, you can now attend. It would make Amy's night."

"Did it not occur to you that a quiet family dinner might be more appropriate?"

"Look, you only turn twenty-one once and it's the perfect opportunity to show people how far she has come."

"Do you not remember what happened at your engagement party last year?" he asked through gritted teeth.

"That's precisely why she needs this, Bradley. To make people realize she is better."

The poor girl was better then. Her collapse that night had nothing to do with drink or drugs, she was having a damn panic attack!

"Is Amy aware that you've arranged something?"

"Of course, darling. It's going to be the social event of the year!"

Shit! His mother really didn't have a clue. No wonder two of her four husbands had met with an early grave, his father included. The woman was the Devil personified, she represented everything he hated about Hollywood. Not that he could turn his back on the person or the place.

"And she is happy with the idea?" he pushed.

"Absolutely! Charles has invited some people he would like you to meet with as well. Something to do with a new script they are working on..."

And there it was. The real reason for her call. The main driver for the entire party. It wasn't about Amy's birthday or improving his sister's fragile public image. It was all about her. As always. Engineering things so that she could get what she wanted and this time it would be his backing on her new husband's current project. To hell with whether her daughter could cope with the social engagement she'd orchestrated in order to get it!

He knew he had to end the call before he said something they'd both regret. But was it any wonder she had to go to such lengths to get him in the same room when he did everything he could to avoid just that?

"Send the details to Lara," he bit out. "I'll be bringing a date."

"Oh, how lo—"

He hung up. He didn't need to hear anymore. He almost felt sorry for committing Carrie to such an event, but there was no way in hell he could get through the entire thing alone without throttling his mother. And declining the invite was not an option, he couldn't leave his sister to fend for herself.

Having Carrie there would give him the perfect reason not to spend too much time in the presence of his mother and her strategically planted guests.

He just had to hope that three days would be enough time for Carrie to get past whatever illness she was suffering. And as for her possible misgivings about his proposal, he would make sure those were long forgotten by then.

He started the engine and pulled away, his mission well and truly mapped out.

CHAPTER THREE

IT WAS A GOOD RUN by Isla's standards. Every time she felt her pace slip, she thought of the list and it acted like an adrenaline shot. As did the realization that it smacked of rising panic on Carrie's part.

She must have seriously started to regret the idea of swapping places as all the possibilities of what could go wrong had occurred to her.

Or rather, all the wonderful ways in which Isla could let her down and ruin her image. Each diabolical scenario making its way as a new rule onto the list.

Carrie clearly saw her as a scruffy, alcohol intolerant, graceless nerd who didn't have the ability to dress herself let alone behave with any decorum.

Well, she would show her!

Hitting the end button on the state of the art treadmill, she took out her earbuds and bounded off, boosted by a new-found sense of determination. She would prove her sister's doubts unnecessary and convince everyone that she was indeed the perfect Carrie. What that meant in the case of Bradley, she tried not to dwell on. The mere hint of him being near her again had her tummy doing somersaults and a telltale throb kick-starting between her legs.

"I see you're feeling better."

No! Isla spun on her heel. "Bradley!"

He stood lounging in the doorway, one leg crossed over the other, shirt unbuttoned at the collar. Every bit of him emanating the sexy and suave pin-up, save for his eyes. His eyes were on fire, the intense heat of his gaze burning right through her, pinning her to the spot.

How long had he been there?

"Seems I'm making a habit of surprising you." The rough edge to his voice sent a thrilling shiver through her spine and alarm bells ringing in her mind.

"Don't you ever knock first?" she blurted.

"I thought we were past that point in our relationship," he said, his eyes leisurely travelling the length of her, a heated reminder of just how skimpy her gear was.

She bent to pick up her towel, desperate to break his concentration and free herself from the intensity of his gaze.

"I'd just rather you didn't see me like this," she said, straightening and doing her damnedest to avoid looking at him, hoping it would give her chance to recover, to don her Carrie-esque mask.

But she couldn't even do that, her eyes refused to obey, sweeping back to him of their own accord. *He's just too bloody attractive!*

"Do you have any idea how hot you look right now?" he said, mirroring her own internal ramblings

Shit. He hadn't moved from the doorway and yet, he might as well have been upon her, the tension emanating across the room almost palpable.

Nervously, she wiped at the sweat from around her neck, and his attention dropped, his eyes flashing as he took in the stroke of the towel against her skin.

"Here, let me give you a hand with that." Pushing off the doorframe, he strode toward her, his eyes fixed on the towel as she lowered it mindlessly to her side.

He can't be serious!

Heat pooled in her lower belly just as fear speared her mind. She knew she couldn't trust herself. Not where this man was concerned.

With her heart pounding in her ears, she watched him advance and swallowed hard.

"I should take a shower," she breathed.

"Not yet you won't."

Taking the towel from her limp hold, he caught up her ponytail with his free hand. "First, let me enjoy this."

He tugged her head back, the move startling her with its force and causing her to gasp out loud. She should have slapped him. Hard. Not arched her back and closed her eyes like the wanton creature she was swiftly becoming.

Sweat trickled down the curve of her outstretched neck and he circled its path with the towel, the rough fabric and soft caress an intoxicating mix.

"Do you know how much I want you right now?" His voice was tight and she realized with arousing satisfaction that he was barely in control himself.

This had to stop.

Now.

At least she had the excuse of being taken by surprise the first time, to let it all happen again was just plain wrong. She still hadn't got hold of Carrie to confess her previous sin, how could she possibly admit to another straight off the bat?

But then, trying to muster the strength to deny him when her body felt more alive than ever…

"We mustn't," she whispered, but her tone was weak and earned her a smile filled with so much promise that her mind melted.

"We must," he insisted as he lowered his head to her neck, his breath tickling at her skin.

The moment his mouth found the sensitized area beneath her ear, she felt the physical reaction in her pants, her readiness for him undeniable.

"Two weeks—" he broke off to nibble at her lobe, his tongue coaxing, his teeth nipping, his breath hot in her ear "—is too long."

She tried to move her head away, to ease his assault on her senses, but he showed her no mercy. Twisting his fist around her hair, he held her firmly where he wanted her.

"It's been hours," she rebuked, the heat in her veins coming through in the strength of her voice as she raised her hands to push him away. But as soon as she came in contact with the hot, hard muscle of his chest, she crumpled. Her hands started moving to caress rather than oppose. She thought of his naked body that morning, knew what was beneath the fabric of the shirt and reveled in the feel of it flexing beneath her.

"Yes, but after two weeks it appears that once in a day is no longer enough," he said into her ear, his breath sending shivers rippling down her body and causing her to give way to a treacherous moan.

"And it seems your body agrees with me," he remarked approvingly, his mouth lowering to her neck once more as he let his teeth graze against her skin.

"Yes," she hissed, her fingers clutching at his chest in brazen desperation, her nails biting viciously through the fabric of his shirt and forcing him to curse.

"Two can play that game, my little minx," he said roughly, tossing the towel aside and releasing her hair so that he could capture her wrists and force them behind her back. Ensnaring them in one hand, he forced her back to the nearest wall and pinned his free hand above her head.

She gazed up at him, her body restrained and excited beyond measure. "How so?"

He gave her a wicked smile in response, the white-hot desire in his gaze making her breathless.

Slowly, he brought the hand down from above her head, seemingly in no rush to instill his revenge.

Or so she thought.

Lazily, he travelled down the side of her face and her pulsating throat, his fingers lighting up her flesh with their feather-light touch while his eyes feasted on her response. He dipped lower, toying with the curve of her collarbone, tracing a path from her center to the tip of her shoulder, before circling delicately down her sides and across her front. All the while, avoiding the parts of her that begged for his touch, his revenge now clear.

She swiftly became a whimpering mess, her body arching almost painfully as she pleaded with him to drop the gentle torture and drive her over the edge.

"I only have to look at you to know how wet you are already," he said, his forehead dipping to meet with her own as he lowered his sights to her chest, his hand now coming to rest upon the exposed skin beneath the band of her top.

Entranced, she followed his gaze and could see for herself that her nipples were like beacons begging for his attention, their hard tips straining against the confines of her top.

"Truly stunning," he whispered and without warning, dropped his head, closing his teeth around one engorged peak before she even knew what he was about. Pleasure so intense ricocheted through her, and she cried out, her body bucking helplessly against him.

"That's my baby," he said, repeating the move, his voice shaking with his own barely suppressed need.

She was past caring now. She was past any rational, Isla-style thought. She needed this crazy, mounting ache satisfied and knew he was the man to do it.

Again.

Releasing his hold over her wrists, he pressed her lower body back against the wall and she tilted her pelvis to him, instinctively exposing her throbbing core to the hard swell of his cock.

"God, yes!" she cried feverishly as he hit her sweet spot, her hands thrusting into his hair to hold his attention on her breasts as she shamelessly took up a rhythm against him, now a total slave to the climax she could feel building within.

She heard Bradley gasp. "Christ, Carrie! I need you!"

But she wasn't Carrie.

She wasn't the one he needed.

Her body froze. Her mind played catch up. The reminder of who he was and who she was having the startling effect of a cold shower.

He lifted his head, his eyes ablaze but questioning as he sensed her sudden shift in mood.

She side-stepped away, grateful for the wall behind her for support. "You really don't need me like this, I stink."

Oh God!

Did she really just use that as an excuse? But to be fair, it was the kind of thing Carrie would say. It wouldn't surprise her if her sister had never let Bradley see her sweat-clad body. All for the same reason she wouldn't work out in public.

"To be frank, you could smell like a sewer right now and it wouldn't put me off," he said, closing the gap she had created. "You must have worked out so much these last two weeks, I've never seen you so toned or so hot."

"I've been working on a new routine," she lied, her voice shaky as she tried to step away once more and found she had run out of space, her side meeting with the mirrored back wall of the gym.

"It's certainly working," he said, scanning her upper body with a gaze so fierce it took her breath away, the appreciation in his tone, catching her off guard. She'd never thought of her abs as appealing to the opposite sex. Or the extra weight around her hips and thighs that came from her unrestrained appetite. But he made her feel like the most desired being on the planet.

Did he prefer how she looked to Carrie?

Don't go there, Isla!

"Look, I really need to take a shower," she moved to go around him but he caught her arm and swung her into his embrace.

"Yes, we can shower together later," he agreed and then his mouth came crushing down on hers, reigniting a desire so wild and all-consuming that there was no room for thought, it was pure sensation. The feel of his tongue as it forced its way into her mouth leading her own into a crazy, hungry dance of taste and touch.

He groaned deep in his throat as she folded into him, her lower body pressing brazenly against him as she sought the friction she had escaped from just moments before.

He tore his mouth away. "Why would you want to forgo this?"

She pulled his head back to hers, her mouth seeking out the onslaught of his, desperate not to think. Her body filled with frustration as it struggled to seek out the sweet spot it had found previously.

It just wasn't enough, she needed more.

As if hearing her thoughts, he reached behind her thighs and forced them apart, lifting her up so that she folded her legs around him, his cock now positioned perfectly against her swollen clit. She moaned her gratitude into his throat, their tongues continuing their frenzied tryst.

She felt him turn, knew he was carrying her somewhere but she didn't care. She just wanted to feel the intense release her body was promising. She felt the hard edge of a table as he set her down, the cushioned softness of what must be the top of the physio table beneath her. And still he kissed her like his life depended on it. This was bigger than anything she had ever known. The one night in college where she'd made such a huge mistake had nothing on this. The episode this morning was still burning through her brain and adding fuel to the intoxicating power he had over her. It was truly terrifying, wonderful, and—

Katy Perry suddenly filled the room, the chorus of *Firework* blaring out.

"Not now!" Bradley stilled, his hand diving into his back pocket, his expression one of rising humility. "It's my sister's idea of a joke," he said by way of explanation, extracting his phone and cutting off the sound. "Next week it will be another mortifying ringtone to announce her call."

Completely dazed, Isla just nodded.

He looked torn, his eyes flicking between her and the phone.

She fought to calm her raging pulse and quash the unwelcome sense of disappointment. She should be grateful; the phone call was her saving grace. "It's okay, you should speak to her."

He debated for a second more, his hand thrusting through his hair in obvious frustration.

"I'll still be around when you're done," she assured him.

"You better." He planted a chaste kiss on the tip of her nose and turned to walk to the window, his fingers working the phone as he called his sister back.

Her body immediately pined for his attention. The cold sense of loss made all the more severe coming straight off the back of such an intense high.

A high she had no right to enjoy.

Angry at herself, she leapt up off the table and grabbed up her towel, pressing it against her face as she felt the sudden sting of tears. She needed to get a grip.

Heading for the door to give him privacy for his call, she felt him turn and he was alongside her in seconds, his hand upon her arm to halt her.

"Stay," he mouthed, his eyes intent on her face, a flicker of concern in their depths. Could he see she was upset?

Unwillingly, she nodded and turned back into the room.

He smiled his gratitude and then piped up into the phone, "Hey, squirt!"

Isla watched him turn away once more and she busied herself with her phone, logging her workout in her app diary and doing her utmost not to eavesdrop but listening all the same.

"Do you really need to insist on calling me that?" his sister asked on the other end of the line, her smile coming through in her tone.

"When you stop sticking embarrassing ringtones on my phone, maybe I'll stop giving you embarrassing nicknames," he said, his own face breaking into a grin despite the throbbing of his cock.

He flicked a glance in Carrie's direction and felt his concentration on the call lapse. He hadn't lied when he'd said she was more appealing than ever. Both her curves and added definition were having a devastating effect on his self-control.

He'd arrived with every intention of checking her wellbeing, delivering the flowers, making sure she had eaten and spending some time in her company. He also needed to put the idea of the party to her. Not to mention, the proposal that still went unanswered.

What he hadn't expected to see was her virtually naked body slick with sweat, her muscles working hard atop the treadmill as she'd rhythmically run at a tempo even he would have struggled to maintain. All the while, his gaze fixated on the cheeks of her bum peeking out of the hot pants that fitted her so tightly they gave no room for underwear. His control had gone the way of his power of speech as he'd found himself rooted to the spot, all thought of announcing his presence forgotten.

"So, she wasn't making it up?" His sister's voice beckoned him back to the call.

"Sorry, sis, what were you saying?" His voice was laced with guilt as he rearranged himself, his pants were becoming increasingly uncomfortable.

Carrie chose that exact moment to look up at him, and she caught the move, her cheeks flushing. He couldn't remember her ever being quite so…so bashful, it intrigued him and he winked at her, the gesture a mixture of fun and a warning of what was to come when he could get off the phone. She averted her gaze, looking almost panicked, and began to toy with her cellphone.

"Mom says that you and her have a party arranged for Friday?"

You *and* mom. No wonder his sister doubted it.

"Yes," he lied, sometimes where their mother and Amy were concerned, it was the best thing.

"Oh," she said, surprise clear in her voice.

"We spoke when I got back early and decided a birthday party would be a good thing for you."

"It is a nice thought, Brad," she paused briefly and he could sense her discomfort, gritting his teeth as he silently cursed their heartless mother for doing this to her. "I'm just not sure I'm in the mood for some big event."

He shoved his hand through his hair and he felt Carrie's gaze narrow on him, clearly detecting his swing in mood.

Turning away from her, he said, "Will it make you feel better if we help with the arrangements?"

"Will you?" she said, the relief in her tone more than evident.

"Of course, together we can reign her in and make it perfect."

"Thank you so much, Brad! She just doesn't take no for an answer and I don't want to let her down."

He had to bite back the words he wanted to utter, his free hand fisting at his side. "It's no trouble at all, and you won't let her down, it's your birthday and it's all about you, honey."

She gave a small laugh. "Does that mean you can come over this evening?" she asked, a bubble of excitement now emerging. "She wants to go through the final arrangements and it would help if you were there."

He glanced at Carrie, thinking of the plans he had envisaged for them and tried to incorporate her into them, keen not to have to be apart once again.

"Of course, what time are you meeting?"

Now he had his sister settled he was keen to pick up where him and Carrie had left off. Especially as the female in question was now bending forward once more. This time to pick up her earphones that had gone the way of her towel earlier, to the floor. Her breasts once again almost forcing their way out of the top that, if he was honest, looked too small for her. He wondered if he should tell her so, but frankly, if she only wore it in his presence then it was a win-win situation.

"Are you still there, Brad?"

Mentally cursing, he tore his gaze from the inviting mounds. "Sure am, what time did you say?"

"Seven thirty."

"No problem, we will see you there."

"We?" she prompted, her curiosity piqued.

"I have a friend I'd like to bring."

"Carrie?" Nothing seemed to pass his sister by. The two hadn't met and he kept his private life close to his chest, so her knowledge was surprising.

"How do you know?"

She went quiet.

"Amy?" His senses prickled as he realized her answer before she even gave it. "Has Lara been speaking to you?"

"Brad, please…" she hesitated, worry clear in her tone.

Damn! He didn't want to upset her.

"I get that you're friends, Amy," he said softly. "But the idea of you discussing my private affairs is plain weird that's all, she's my employee at the end of the day."

"It's not like that. Not really. I think she just likes to…you know, share."

"Well enough *sharing* about me, okay? Lara needs to remember she works for me, there is a professional line that shouldn't be crossed."

"Please don't blame Lara, Brad. It's my fault too. Us girls just like to gossip, that's all."

"Yes, I forget how you girls like to talk," he teased. "Reminds me why you are all such a pain in the ass."

"Hey, asswipe! I'd slap you for that one if you were here."

"No, you wouldn't, you need my help too much."

"Ain't that the truth," she admitted, her voice quietly nervous.

"Stop stressing, it's going to be great," he assured her. "We'll see you this evening."

"Thanks, Brad! I love you."

His heart warmed. "Love you too, squirt."

"*Brad!*"

He cut the phone off and smiled, his eyes re-finding Carrie, or more specifically, her tight ass as she bent over the weights stack, scanning her own phone with her back to him.

He strode toward her, his groin primed and ready, his hands itching to take hold of the cheeks peeking tantalizing out from beneath the hem of her hot pants. He was upon her before she reacted to his approach, her body tensing as he took hold of her hips to turn her into him.

"Hi," she said, peeking up at him, her bashful persona firmly in place. She was a bag of contradiction and he was struggling to keep up. His nagging cock wasn't making it any easier to concentrate either.

He smiled at her, his brain ordering his groin to stand down long enough to make her relax. "Sorry about that. Amy's having a panic as Marie's arranged a birthday party for her this Friday."

She studied him. "It's sweet of you to offer to help."

"What else can I do, leaving her to deal with our mother on her own would be like throwing a lamb to the slaughter," he said candidly, glad that he didn't need to put on a front where Carrie was concerned, as she knew it all. "She's my little sister and probably the one good thing Marie ever managed to bring into my life."

"She is lucky to have you looking out for her."

"Even better than that, she has *us* looking out for her."

"Us?" she asked, her eyebrows raising in surprise.

"Yes, I've just committed us to help plan the event, her and Marie are going through it tonight and she wants us to help keep her in check. I assume you'll be happy to help."

"I can't come tonight."

He frowned. "Why?"

"I have things I need to do."

"Things?" he balked. "Please, Carrie, I could do with a female brain on this party planning exercise and I don't particularly want to use my PA. Lara's knowledge of my private life is teetering on the brink of her role as it is thanks to her friendship with my sister. And to be honest, exposing her to the bitch that is my mother, isn't really part of her job description."

"So, you want to throw me in there instead?" she asked, eyebrows raised even higher.

"Well, you, babe…" he dropped his head to rest against her forehead, his eyes lowering to the appealing curve of her mouth as he remembered how she had tasted minutes before. "You need to get used to the woman sooner or later."

"Is that so?" she whispered, her teeth worrying her bottom lip, the move tantalizingly erotic to his piped-up cock.

"Please?" Now he couldn't work out if he was saying please to her accepting the invite or please to throwing her back against the physio table and fucking her senseless.

"Okay." She was so quiet he wasn't sure he'd heard her correctly.

"You will?"

"Yes."

A buzzing started up and automatically, he went for his phone. Carrie did the same.

"It's me," she said, lifting the vibrating device to check the screen. Her eyes lit up and she pressed the device to her chest, concealing the display from him. "I need to take this."

"That's okay, I can wait." He didn't care much for her excitement over the caller. *Is it a guy?*

"No, you go," she insisted, her free hand coming up to press against his chest and reinforcing her words. "I'll take this call and then I'll see you later. What time do you need me ready?"

He wanted to argue, to stay, but ultimately she was doing what he wanted by coming with him that evening. He needed to focus on that.

"I'll pick you up about seven."

"Great, you can walk yourself out," she said, grabbing up her towel and making for the door. Her head clearly on the caller as she issued the flippant dismissal.

He didn't like it.

Not one bit.

"Hey, not so fast!" He caught her arm to halt her. "I'm not leaving without a proper goodbye, minx."

Pulling her back against him hard, his mouth claimed hers with brutal intent, his purpose to remind her that he couldn't be so easily dismissed.

She moaned a protest even as her body turned to liquid in his hands, her focus once more gratifyingly on him as her mouth surrendered to his kiss, her tongue needing no encouragement.

He wanted to leave her wanting, her body primed for him and him alone. He wanted to be sure that he was the one on her mind when she dealt with the caller, whomever it was.

He could hear the vibrating again and realized with satisfaction that she was oblivious. He had her. His displeasure at her easy dismissal enough to keep his own control in check. Just.

He set her away from him.

"Your caller is persistent." His tone was hard but taking in her dazed state, he couldn't help the smile that formed. She wanted him. Bad.

"Off you go," he commanded.

She took a moment to react. Her cheeks flushing and her eyes glittering. She dropped her gaze to the phone and it shocked her into the present. She didn't look at him as she swiftly turned away, the words "I'll see you at seven" being issued to the doorway rather than himself.

His smile spread as he watched her flee.

Her body was like a shaken Champagne bottle, fit to pop for him at any moment, and he couldn't wait. The anticipation of the explosion that he knew was brewing kept him hard long after she had broken away.

One thing was for sure, she would be screaming his name before the night was out.

CHAPTER FOUR

ISLA RACED UPSTAIRS, THE BITTER taste of betrayal stuck in her throat. How could she have let herself go like that? *Again?*

It was a bloody stupid question.

The very idea that she could resist Bradley King himself was laughable and yet, to succumb to his charms while living out a lie was just plain wrong.

The phone was still ringing when she entered the bedroom, her phone number flashing on the lit screen. She needed to answer it but she didn't dare. Not until she was sure he had left and she'd had chance to wash away the incriminating flush from her skin.

Tossing her gym towel to the bed, she freed her hands to issue Carrie a text: *Will call you in ten minutes—do not disappear!* Ix

The response, *OK, Cx*, came back almost immediately.

She stripped and showered, the water tepid in a vain attempt to ease the top-to-toe ache. She had wanted him—bad. Even now, with him gone, the memory of his presence burned through her, her ears filling with the arousing resonance of his voice, her swollen lips still buzzing from his parting kiss, the throb between her legs, just as intense and unyielding.

She upped the ferocity of the water flow, keen to beat him away. Instead, her body reveled in the head-on onslaught. The sharp jets of water triggering shoots of pleasure as her mind defiantly replayed the feel of his mouth on her skin, his fingers on her back and in her hair, his vice-like grip upon her wrists as he'd held her captive and wanting.

She caught sight of her reflection in the mirrored wall: her face flushed and startlingly unrecognizable; her body arched as she offered herself up to the punishing flow; her breasts demanding as the hardened peaks at their center craved every wet lashing.

What was happening to her? When had she become this sex-crazed and alive?

She'd considered herself immune to the opposite sex, her protective shield put in place years ago, now very much part of who she was. What had initially started as avoidance of her sister's fallen victims had become an avoidance of men in general. Add to that the failure of her parents' once-perfect marriage and she was destined to be a spinster.

Except *he* had come into her life. And *he* was everything she shouldn't want.

She didn't need the passion, she didn't yearn for the excitement, and she certainly didn't crave the pain or complication that accompanied her sister's conquests, past or present.

She would never go there again.

Her body burned with the humiliating reminder of her messed-up past, and she used it to fuel her temper, stamping out the remnants of desire and giving her a much-needed focus. She hurried through the remainder of her shower, and turned her thoughts to the impending conversation with Carrie. Boy, was she in for a drilling!

Wrapping a towel around her hair and body, she returned to the bedroom and took up the phone. Propping it on the dressing table before her, she triggered a video call and waited.

Carrie answered in two rings, her perfectly dressed face filling the screen, her forehead creased in concern. "Isla, you okay?"

"What do you think?" she snapped back, she couldn't help it, her body was wound so tightly she needed to feel the release of taking it out on someone.

Carrie's eyes narrowed on her. "Have you just boiled yourself in the shower? You look like a lobster." Settling back from the screen, she wrinkled her little nose. "It's really not a good look."

Any scrap of patience expired with her sister's critical words and, fisting her palms atop the table, Isla gave way to her rant: "Yes, I've taken a shower, but believe me, the color of my skin has sod all to do with your water temperature, and everything to do with the heat of your sex-life."

Her sister frowned. "I don't know what you're talking about."

"Don't lie to me, Carrie! How could you think not to tell me?"

Now it was Carrie's turn to go pink, the color glowing through despite the layers of expertly applied makeup and fake tan. "How did you find out? Did mum say something?"

"Mum?" Isla returned, her anger stoked. "You mean mum knew and still you didn't think to tell me? Christ, Carrie! The guy turned up in my—I mean, *your* bed…while I was in it…asleep!"

Carrie took a moment to register her words, a flurry of emotions passing over her face before horror dawned. "Oh my God, Isla! I am so sorry! He wasn't supposed to be back for another month or so. I didn't think to tell you because I didn't think you needed to know."

"So, you didn't think your sister should know that you are in a relationship. And not with just anyone—*with him*? We're supposed to tell each other everything, I should have been the first person you told!"

"I didn't feel comfortable telling you, not when I wasn't sure where it was heading"—her sister scraped a hand down her increasingly worried face—"it felt like rubbing your nose in it unnecessarily."

"So, instead I have to find out by waking up to a stranger in the same bed?" If her voice went any higher only the dogs would be able to hear her. "I kicked him in the nuts, Carrie! His *naked* nuts! Do you know how humiliating that was?"

To Isla's satisfaction, her sister's skin flushed deeper, and fired up by her reaction she carried on, "Never mind the fact that I've been unable to avoid the intimacy your relationship demands, the guy is on heat I sw—"

"You *haven't*!" Carrie blurted over her, her mouth falling agape.

Isla stilled. She needed to say it, but the words just rolled around her head, her tongue becoming too thick to form a single vowel, her head humming with the dizzying extremity of what she had to own up to.

Turns out she needn't have worried, her twin's ability to read her silent confession via the minute phone screen had it covered. "I see," Carrie acknowledged eventually, her head nodding slowly as she took on board the revelation.

"You see?" Isla repeated dumbly, her guilty gaze struggling to maintain contact with the screen as she waited for the fireworks to hit.

"Yes, I do," Carrie said, her voice now strong but far from mad, her face morphing into one of absolute calm.

What the fuck?

Her sister was an exceptional actress, she was great at what she did, but it was damn right eerie watching it for real and Isla was lost for words as she questioned the sincerity of her composure.

"Well," Carrie continued with a dismissive shrug, "I can't say I'm surprised…I mean, what else could you do in that situation?"

She wasn't acting, Isla realized in amazement. She genuinely thought this was okay.

Isla should have been relieved, pleased, even…instead, she was utterly pissed. "You mind telling me why you're so goddamn cool about this?"

"I'm not cool, I'm just accepting it as a *fait accompli*," her sister said, waving an airy-fairy hand about.

"A *fait accompli?*" Isla snorted in disbelief.

"Absolutely! It's not like you had the advantage of advance warning, and I know first-hand how hard he is to resist."

Isla's tummy turned over, she didn't want to think about him seducing Carrie, and she certainly didn't want reminding that she was once again second dibs.

If she hadn't realized it before, she certainly did now: there was no way she could do this anymore, not to him and not to herself. She'd been foolish to think otherwise.

"So, you'll understand if I end this charade then, sis?" Isla saw Carrie visibly tense, but she continued regardless, her voice determined. "I can't pretend, not to him."

"*Please, you have to!*" her sister pleaded, the sudden crack in her cool taking Isla by surprise. "I *need* people to believe you are me."

"I'm not saying I won't keep up the pretense in public, there's no reason for all and sundry to know I'm not you, but he is your..." She struggled for the right word, unable to bring herself to use *boyfriend* or any other such love-evoking term, going with what she could stomach. "He is your partner, he should know."

"It's not that simple."

Isla shook her head in frustration. "It really is, Carrie."

"Look, it's hard for him to trust women as it is, I don't want him knowing that we came up with this idea. He'll hate the falsity of it all."

"Are you shitting me? You live in a world that feeds on lies and deceit, it's second nature, surely!"

Carrie reacted as though slapped. "Well, that's a bit harsh."

Isla knew she was getting carried away and letting age-old family issues rear their ugly head, but in that moment, she didn't care. "You know my feelings on Hollywood, Carrie, it shouldn't be a surprise to you."

"Yes, and I still stand by what I said, you're being unfair..." Her sister looked like she would say more on the subject but then sighed, her eyes lowering as she said, "I don't want to argue about this with you. I'm sorry I didn't tell you everything, but life has gotten really complicated of late and I've been struggling to think straight. I know it's no excuse, but I never meant to upset you."

Her sister sounded genuinely contrite and verging on tears; it had Isla's anger deflating like a popped balloon. "I don't get you, Carrie, I tell you I've slept with your bloke and you hardly react, I tell you I'm pissed at you and that I hate the world you live in, and you fold."

"Like I said, it's complicated. Part of me wanting to come back here was about seeing past the glitz and glamor of Hollywood life, to try and get a handle on what's truly important to *me*. To work out, what it is *I* really want."

"Okay, I get that," Isla said. "But why does that mean I have to lie to him, surely he will understand if you just explain like you have done me?"

"No," her sister stressed. "I can't. It'll cause more problems than it's worth right now."

Isla studied her, this conversation was getting more and more incredulous by the second. "So, what exactly are you suggesting I do then? Roll around in the sack with him until you get back and hope that our sexual nuances don't give me…us…away?"

Carrie flinched, and Isla ignored the spark of guilt. She knew she was being deliberately crude but she didn't know how else to get the message across.

"There's no need to be so graphic about it," her sister started.

"There's every reason," Isla said firmly. "You should know full well how high his sex-drive is, you want to tell me how I go about rebuking him without landing you and your relationship in it?"

Carrie's color deepened. "Just avoid him. At least, until I get back. He has a rammed schedule, so I can't imagine he will be sticking around for long, just make excuses—"

"You mean, more lies?"

"I know, Isla, but I need the space, space without him in it right now."

"This is crazy! I can't avoid him. In fact, I'm committed to going out with him this evening, his mother has organized a party for his sister Amy, and—"

"She's done what?" her sister interjected sharply.

"Bradley said it was for her birthday," Isla said simply, startled by her sister's emotive response. "But apparently Amy is stressing that their mother will get carried away with the planning so he volunteered me…you…to help."

"What the hell is Marie playing at?"

The source of their argument momentarily forgotten, Isla shrugged. "I thought a birthday party was a nice thing to do for someone."

"Yes, it's nice when it's something they will enjoy," Carrie agreed, her brows knitted together. "But when the guest of honor is a recovering druggy with a fear of relapsing so powerful that she collapsed at her last social event, it's plain thoughtless."

"Oh my God, poor girl!"

"And poor Brad," her sister said, her concern ringing through. "This is going to be killing him."

"Well, it's just another good reason to end this charade now, at least where he is concerned, he has enough to deal with."

Her sister finally had the decency to look guilty. "I can't."

"What do you mean you can't?"

"It's *complicated*."

If she heard her sister say "it's complicated" one more time she was going to break something. "You're going to have to go one better than 'it's complicated', sis."

"It just is, Isla, please take my word for it. Right now, Brad is going to need me there to support him, but I can't be there. And I can't give away where I am without telling him stuff that I need to explain to him in person."

"Then call him, and speak to him directly. You can tell him you can't make this evening and that you are going back home for a bit, sending me in your place to keep the press off you. It's not the complete truth, but it's better than telling him it's me he's been...been..." Isla couldn't finish the sentence, the unspoken words had her tummy churning and her cheeks ablaze.

"I can't." Her sister's face scrunched up in thinly veiled panic. "I'm not ready for that conversation."

"Ready for *what* conversation?" she pushed, completely baffled by her sister's continued refusal. "You just tell him you're taking some time out to evaluate your life. What's so difficult about that?"

Their gazes locked via the phone screen, Isla's steely resolve well and truly in place, while her sister—the faultless, unshakeable Carrie—was alarmingly on edge, her nervous cheek-chomping screaming of something far more problematic.

"Tell me what's really going on," Isla pushed eventually, softening her tone in the hope it would coax Carrie into speaking up. "Look, I *know* you, and I know that there is more to this than what you are telling me."

Patiently, she waited, making it clear to Carrie that this conversation wasn't going anywhere until she was completely honest with her.

Eventually her sister reacted, her cheeks puffing outward on a gust of air, the gesture so unflattering it teased a smile out of Isla. "Christ, it must be bad if you feel capable of pulling that face."

Carrie didn't so much as smile at her sisterly insult, instead she leaned toward the phone screen as she whispered, "He proposed."

He proposed. He proposed. He proposed. The words bounced around Isla's mind, waiting to hit a nerve, to actually sink in.

"Seriously, Isla," her sister stressed. "He proposed and I didn't know what to do."

Bullseye! Isla's heart and mind took the hit. A rush of emotion swept through her; bitterness, betrayal, secrecy, jealousy...all manner of hurt kicking her in the gut and leaving her winded. She couldn't speak. She couldn't think.

"Did you hear me, Isla?"

"I heard you," she said, her voice deadly quiet. "I'm just struggling to process it."

"I'm sorry, I know I should have told you," her sister hurried out, her words tumbling one after another. "But in truth, it was a huge shock when it happened and on paper it's perfect, how could I tell you and expect you to understand my hesitancy."

"Hesitancy?"

"Yes, you won't get it," her sister continued. "After all, he's a successful actor-cum-director-cum-production company owner. He has the power to let me be whoever I want to be, for as long as I want to do it. And he is a great man too. Trustworthy. Gorgeous. Amazing in bed—"

"Yes, you're right, on paper it's the perfect match for you," she cut in bitterly, desperate to have her sister shut up. She couldn't bear to listen to it.

"But…" Carrie began and then paused.

Isla stared daggers at her. Could her sister really be telling her that there was a "but"?

"See, you're doing it now! You're judging me!" Carrie accused.

Could Isla deny it?

No. She *was* judging her.

She was branding her self-obsessed. She was deeming her unchanged from her teenage days, when she'd had it all and still it hadn't been enough. No matter who she hurt in the process, she had to have more.

She was just like dear old dad.

"You don't need me to judge you, Carrie, I think you're doing a pretty good job of that yourself." The words were like acid in her throat.

"You don't understand, Isla."

"I understand perfectly. You bewitched him, he fell in love, he proposed, and you ran."

"No."

"*Yes*! You gave me this crap about it being a good idea for me to get away with my business folding and gave me the sob story about how you needed a break from the public eye, but all the time you wanted to escape another love-crazed buffoon."

"Isla, stop it!" It was her sister's turn to be angry. "He is no buffoon. And he is *not* in love with me."

"Of course he is."

"No, if you let me finish, I will explain."

Isla's mind was spinning, she was so angry. Angry at him for being taken as a fool, for wearing his heart on his sleeve and having his sister walk all over him.

She was angry at her sister for doing it to yet another guy, her selfish traits prevailing once again.

She was angry with herself for the unbidden jealousy that coursed through her, making a mockery of her anti-relationship stance.

"I can't talk about this any more right now," she said, her voice shaking.

"Isla, please, if I explain then hopefully you will under—"

"Save it, Carrie."

"*Please.*"

"I'll call you when I'm ready to talk."

Carrie looked like she would stop her again. She could see the tears pricking in her sister's eyes and knew she had hurt her.

Quashing the guilt that threatened to take hold, Isla moved to end the call.

"Wait!" Carrie blurted, her hand raised to the phone screen as if to stop her.

Isla paused. "What?"

"Please, promise me you won't tell him, not yet. Just help him get through the party and I promise I will get my head together."

"Don't worry, I have no desire to tell a man that the woman he loves has legged it and left him with her second-rate sister."

She expected Carrie to at least give her a token denial of her inferiority. Something to try and make her feel better. Instead her sister was distracted, her attention drawn to a sound in the background as she turned away from the screen. "Tell him I'll be down in five minutes."

Isla's ears burned just as Carrie's focus came back to the call.

"What was that all about?'

Carrie's face flushed for the umpteenth time that call. "Just mum."

Isla nodded. "I make it eight in the evening your way, who's the guy that needs you at this time of night?"

Her sister's flawless skin burned deeper. "It's Dan."

"So, all day out with him, and now all night too?" she said, a shard of ice spearing her heart, memories returning to haunt her. "I can really see how you are using your time well to work out your relationship issues."

"Isla—"

"Bye, sis."

Isla ended the call and shut her eyes tight, waiting for the threat of tears to subside. She would not spill another over the same battleground. It simply wasn't worth it.

And if Dan was stupid enough to become ensnared once more, then more fool him. She had a much healthier coping strategy brewing, one that had her body readily purring in anticipation.

CHAPTER FIVE

BRAD HAD MENTALLY ALLOCATED AN hour to being in his mother's company.

That hour had expired forty-five minutes ago and the three women were showing little sign of being ready to wrap it up. In fact, he might as well have not been there.

He watched in amazement as they huddled together on the couch opposite him. Their heads bent over what he'd been told, rather than shown, were catering menus, their voices laced with excitement. Even his mother had an energy about her. Although that could have more to do with the upcoming meeting between him and Charles. He pushed the bitter thought aside, happy to pretend for at least the next few days that they were one happy family.

"I wouldn't choose these, not if you want people to feel comfortable eating them in their finest," Carrie was saying, circling an area of a page. "But these, on the other hand, clean to eat and really fill a hole. They also look good on the serving dish."

Her animated gestures and flurry of words portrayed a passion for food he'd not seen in her before. He'd always believed her to eat out of necessity rather than enjoyment. Always careful to stick to what she knew and only in small amounts. But the girl opposite him had spent most of the evening waxing lyrical about explosive flavor combinations, unusual dishes to surprise and excite, and appropriate drink pairings that had to be tried. She had them all enraptured.

He watched her now, sat between his mother and sister, her attire completely out of place and subtly righted himself. There was nothing sexy about what she was wearing. Her plain white T-shirt scooped high at the neck, only hinting at the appealing swell of her breasts. Her light stonewashed jeans may cling tight from her ass to her ankles, but positioned as she was, her legs folded beneath her upon the couch, it was only the memory of watching her walk to and from the car that teased him with that fact.

No, there was something different about her. A real warmth. It radiated from her with every word she spoke or move she made.

His surprise when she had casually kicked off her sneakers to tuck her feet under her bottom had almost ended in his wine glass emptying itself into his lap. As for Marie, he thought his mother was going to faint, but in all fairness, she had recovered well, her days in acting school many eons ago not an entire waste of time.

And to give Carrie her dues, her assumed position, almost childlike as it was, did make it easier for her to pore over the party paraphernalia without hindering Marie and Amy's view.

He smiled to himself. He couldn't remember the last time he had dared have his feet up on the furniture, even in his own domain. But to see Carrie do it, so engrossed in what they were discussing, had been endearing. She didn't even seem aware of doing it. She would probably die of shame if she knew. At least she had slipped off the white sneakers she wore first.

His eyes dropped to the footwear sitting neatly at the foot of the couch. In truth, he hadn't believed Carrie possessed such an ensemble, accustomed as he was to the heels and designer clothes that always spoke of her affluence. Not that he minded the high-end wear, she worked hard for what she bought and part of her role in life was to always look the part. But it was good, real good, to see her like this.

"Ooo, what are these? I like these," Amy piped up, her eyes bright and skin flushed, her body leaning into Carrie with such trust and affection, it was hard to believe they had never met before. They were clearly destined to be firm friends.

It was another bonus. Another reason why he had to make his proposal come off. He just needed to pin Carrie down and get her to make a decision.

Hollywood could be a lonely place, especially when you'd been burned enough times. It was one of the reasons they'd been drawn together. What had started as a wild night at a party, both of them having drunk too much, confessed a lot and gone too far, had quickly evolved into a friendship with perks.

They cared for one another. It wasn't love, not in the traditional sense. Neither felt that to be truly attainable in Hollywood. But they still craved the companionship of a relationship, and being "off the market" had many benefits. Sure enough, you would still get harangued by would-be lays out for no good, but the word "no" had more impetus when one could flash a ring at them. After all, everyone loves a happy Hollywood couple that makes it work. No matter if under the surface it's based purely on good sex and friendship.

Carrie chose that moment to glance up at him and her cheeks flared, a shy smile creeping across her face. It was a look he was starting to become familiar with and he returned it easily, his eyes intent on her as he tried to read the thoughts going through her mind.

Was she remembering the spanking he had delivered earlier that morning, or the unfinished business in the gym? Or was she thinking on the impenetrable tension that had filled the car on their journey over? They had spent it in an uncomfortable silence. Each time he'd attempted a conversation, she'd given him a monosyllabic answer, discouraging any further communication. He had upped the music and respected her desire to remain wrapped up in her thoughts, but whatever they had been, they'd been far from relaxing. She had wrung her hands so tightly, he'd worried she'd be sporting bruises by the time they had arrived.

Perhaps she'd been fighting the same desire he had: to park the car and finish what they had started that afternoon. His ego would like to think that, but something in her mood when he had collected her suggested it was more serious. To look at her now, though, he wondered if he'd read too much into it.

"Wouldn't you agree, Bradley?"

Carrie's question jarred him back to the matter at hand and he cleared his throat, shifting in his seat. All three ladies now looked to him expectantly and he had no idea what he was supposed to be responding to. "Agree? To what?"

Her smile grew. Was she working out that she was the cause of his preoccupation? Was he being that obvious?

"Wouldn't you say that we should cap the guest list at thirty?" she asked him lightly.

He saw his mother grimace out of the corner of his eye, her desperation to overrule evident.

"It's short notice," Carrie continued, doing an excellent job of ignoring his mother's anxiety, "and we want to be sure we can provide a high-quality affair fitting for Amy's twenty-first. Keeping the list restricted gives us the best chance of creating the right atmosphere."

Carrie's eyes were trained on him and told him a very different reasoning to what she said aloud. This was all about protecting Amy.

She knew, as did everyone else in the room, that if they threw enough money at it, the party would be a spectacular affair regardless of numbers.

Spectacular for everyone but Amy.

His heart warmed while his cock pulsed, the urge to both hug and ravish her taking hold. He may not love her, but she was starting to evoke feelings that ran a whole lot deeper than he believed possible. It should have worried him, in fact it would have worried him a few weeks ago, but now, as he looked across at her, all sweet and relaxed in his family home, he rather liked the idea.

"Sounds reasonable to me," he said, his voice thick even to his own ears.

His mother shot him a disapproving stare. "Really, Bradley, I do think sixty would be far more acceptable in our circles."

He could see Amy visibly tensing, her skin losing its glow of moments before and he wanted to throttle Marie. Instead, he gave her a hard look. "I believe you have certain people you would like in attendance, mother. By my reckoning, six guests of your specific choosing should be enough. That gives you a fifth of the guest list."

His meaning was clear. If she shut up and let thirty stick, he would give time to the people she wanted him to meet. Push and it would be game over before they even begin.

His mother gave a flustered shrug of her shoulders and nodded. "Very well, thirty it is."

Amy relaxed back into the couch and Carrie gave him a triumphant smile, the warmth in her eyes holding his own captive. She had orchestrated the entire planning session with barely any intervention from him. Her ability to read Amy and guide every decision his sister's way had been masterful. No upset, no major disagreement, no unhappy women in his life. Perfect.

Or at least it would be perfect, if he could get Carrie the hell out of there and show her his gratitude in private!

She could read him like a book and ground her bottom into her feet beneath her, trying to ease her body's reaction. How could his sister and mother not see it? Not feel it? It was all she could do not to sidle over and slip her legs about him.

But the pair seemed totally oblivious. Their chatter unperturbed by the thickness in the air, the very real charge to the atmosphere, and the audible pounding of her heart as it banged in her chest at an uncontrollable rate.

They were choosing guests now. She knew that. Amy to the left would list someone and Marie to the right would add it to the list or do her best to veto. They didn't need her for this. She had done her bit and Bradley was pleased. She could see his gratitude in his smile. But his eyes…his eyes were saying something else entirely. It went along the lines of "I want to fuck you, right now".

She sucked back a breath as she forced down a reciprocal moan, her body crying out to do just as his eyes demanded. She wriggled her toes under her, her fingers taking up a tempo on her knees, anything to keep her mind focused on an action, anything to soothe and distract. She flicked a glance at the clock. Would they leave soon?

She saw Bradley catch the move and his smile grew. "I think we've about nailed this party planning for this eve, so if you guys don't mind, I'll take Carrie home."

Home. She swallowed. Was that Carrie's home or his home? And what was she going to do? She had set out on a mission tonight. To feed the desire still coursing through her, and to say to hell with Carrie and her rules. She had chucked on her slobs with sneakers in outright defiance of her sister and regretted it as soon as her butt hit the seat of his spaceship; whatever car it was, its doors that flipped up were not designed to admit a nobody like her. And the four walls of the house they were in now certainly didn't see people like her unless they were employed to service it.

She had been brash and her bluster had all but left her by the time they had arrived. Yes, he had the ability to drive her body swiftly to the brink and make her forget the truth of her situation, but the screaming affluence surrounding her was a reality check she just couldn't ignore. It had been a blessing to get onto the familiar ground of parties and catering. Even if it had to be conducted in his intoxicating presence, her vast knowledge and experience, not to mention her passion for the topic, had her wrapped up in a comfort blanket and she had flourished under it. But now, the planning was coming to end…

"Of course, Bradley," Marie said, pulling Isla back to the present. "It has been very kind of you both to help."

"Yes, it has!" Amy said, surprising Isla as she swung her arms about her neck and squeezed tightly, the girl's cropped chocolate hair tickling under her chin as she pressed her head to Isla's collarbone. "Thank you so much, Carrie!"

"It was no bother, I enjoyed it," Isla said, hugging her back and doing her best not to flinch at the mention of her sister's name. She hated misleading people. It was okay from a distance, as a publicity stunt; not lying as such, just a swift public outing here and there. That's what this swap was supposed to have been about, but it was way more than that now. She was getting to know these people, and the more time she spent with them, the bigger the lie was becoming.

"Can I ask you a favor?" Amy asked, releasing her hold to give her the full weight of her pretty pixie features, her small oval face upturned so that she could cajole her with her excited blue gaze.

Isla couldn't help but smile and nod.

"Will you come dress shopping with me tomorrow? Lara is supposed to be coming but she has to work"—she rolled her eyes at Bradley—"so she might only be able to see us at lunch, and I always take for-*freaking*-ever to find something I like. It will take the day, at least!"

"Of course I will," Isla agreed, before she had the chance to mentally talk herself out of it. The last thing she wanted to do was burst the girl's bubble, even if it did mean pushing her nerves and guilt to the brink as she spent the day in full-on Carrie mode.

"Right, that's settled then," Bradley announced, rising off the sofa. "I'll swing by with Carrie about nine-thirty in the morning for you, squirt."

It was lucky Isla was still sitting. If she hadn't, she may have collapsed. A full day with Amy *and* Bradley…

"You're going to come?" Isla said, trying to sound casual.

"Brad! Don't be ridiculous! You can't come dress shopping!" Amy exclaimed, unwittingly coming to her rescue.

Bradley's eyebrows soared in mock hurt. "Are you saying I don't have exceptional taste in clothing?"

"It's nothing to do with your dress sense," Amy said on a giggle. "It's all about girl time. And *you* are no girl!"

"I sure hope not," he grinned. "In that case, I will resign myself to being your designated driver, I have some stuff I need to get done in the office tomorrow so I can drop you on Melrose Avenue on the way. My SUV could do with a run out."

"Aw, that would be awesome!" Amy bobbed up off the sofa to pin her brother with a suffocating hug, one which he returned just as affectionately. He wore his love for his sister on his sleeve, it was heart-warming and soul-destroying in one fell swoop. The more she discovered about the real him, the more she questioned her prejudiced views of Hollywood and the people that lived in it. And the nicer she found him, the bigger the guilt. Guilt at her duplicity, guilt at being privy to such private moments, and guilt at the feelings she could see she was evoking in not just him but his sister too, forming bonds that she had no right to and wouldn't be sticking around to maintain.

Her head started to swim and she pushed herself off the sofa, trying to distract herself by making to leave, but as she stuffed her feet into her sneakers, the realization that she had sat with her feet on the sofa hit her. She had been so wrapped up in the excitement of the party planning that she hadn't even thought about taking up the position she readily adopted at home. But his mother, she would have picked up on it for sure. She couldn't bring herself to glance the woman's way as she righted herself. It was bad enough that Isla had half expected her to refuse her entry on appearance alone, her distaste for Isla's attire being more than apparent when she'd appeared on her doorstep. But thankfully her negative reception had been drowned out by Amy's sheer delight at their presence. And to give Marie her credit, she had swiftly put aside her displeasure as soon as talk had turned to the party, giving both Isla and Amy her full attention.

The woman herself stood now to stand alongside Isla, and held out her hand. "Thank you for coming, Carrie, it was lovely to see you again."

Isla faltered at the "again" reference—when had she last seen Carrie? Did they see each other often? What did she think of the real Carrie?

Doing her best to conceal her uneasiness, she met the other woman's eye and gently shook her hand. "You're very welcome, Marie."

"Your help has been invaluable," she said, although her voice lacked warmth and her blue eyes, the color of her son and daughter's, narrowed on her, giving Isla the uncomfortable feeling that she was being assessed and found wanting. "I will see you Friday evening, if not before."

Friday evening? Isla sent Bradley a surprised look. She hadn't even thought as far ahead as the actual party, but now his mother had said it, it was obvious—of course they would expect her to attend.

"Sorry for not asking, Carrie." His brow furrowed. "I just assumed..."

"Of course, no, don't be silly, I just hadn't figured it into my plans," she nodded, trying to instill some confidence into her tone. "I'm looking forward to it."

Bradley released Amy and maneuvered around the coffee table toward her, drowning out her concerns with a tide of excitement as his palm met with the small of her back, the contact sending heat searing through the fabric of her T-shirt and setting fire to her pelvic floor.

"We'll see ourselves out," he said to Marie, his voice devoid of any emotion as he leaned forward to deliver a peck on the older woman's awaiting cheek.

"I will send you the attendee list to go over prior to Friday," his mother offered, her hand coming to rest on his chest.

He stepped back immediately, breaking the contact. "No need, so long as Amy and you are happy, I will be too."

A brief flash of pain marred his mother's perfectly sculpted face, but she didn't say anything, her hand dropping back to her side as she turned to Isla. "Enjoy your trip with my daughter tomorrow." The sudden chill in her tone matched the cold of her smile and Isla stifled a shudder. She really didn't want to be on the bad side of this woman.

"Oh, we will!" Amy buzzed behind her. "I'm sure that with Carrie's help I'll find the perfect outfit."

"I'll do my best," Isla said, trying to ignore the fact that Marie now looked like she'd swallowed a wasp; she was clearly delighted that Amy would be taking advice from her—*not!*

"Come, I'll see you both out," Amy said gleefully, hooking her arm in Isla's and practically skipping them out of the room. "Don't worry about mom," she whispered under her breath as she pulled open the grand entrance door. "She has her moments, particularly when the attention isn't on her, but she'll get over it."

Isla nodded skeptically as she stepped out into the heat of the night. It was sweet of the girl to try and reassure her, even if she didn't quite believe what she said.

"Plus, you have my big brother all puppy-eyed," Amy carried on, giving her brother a teasing nudge in the arm. "That will have her totally freaked!"

"Is that so?" Isla said, unable to stop the smile creeping into her cheeks. All puppy-eyed, she said. Had he not been like that before? It was an interesting question…one that she shouldn't really be thinking about but she was anyway…

"Beat it, squirt!" Bradley gave his sister a playful shove back into the house. "Less of the lovey-dovey stuff!"

Amy giggled and rolled her eyes, spinning on her heel. "Whatever you say, Brad, catch ya tomorrow!"

They watched her dance off and Isla felt an overwhelming sense of admiration for the girl that had clearly come a long way if what Carrie had said was true. "She's a cracking kid."

Brad smiled, his expression thoughtful. "She sure is, and she certainly likes you," he said, bringing his sights back to Isla and making her breath catch with the emotion she could read there. "What can I say, we clearly have exceptional taste."

Happiness welled at his compliment, guilt hot on its tail, and she had to look away. "You're very sweet."

"Lord, don't you start," he moaned playfully, pulling the door closed and gesturing for her to precede him to the car. She did so promptly, her eyes fixed to the floor as she battled with her thoughts, her nerves starting to churn. She wanted the courage back from the afternoon, the feisty Isla that didn't give a damn about anything other than getting her rocks off and pissing off her sister.

The spaceship door swung up and, dutifully, she dropped inside, her hands reaching blindly for the seatbelt and fastening it around her. She could feel her insides jittering with her rising anxiety and she tried to take a steadying breath. Next to her, Bradley climbed in, pulling his door closed. Any moment now he would look at her and if she didn't get a hold on herself, she was going to freak him the fuck out.

Pressing her hands into her knees, she pushed herself upright and let go of another breath.

As she expected, Bradley glanced across and she could sense his frown. "Sorry that was such an ordeal."

She forced a smile, eager to put him at ease. She hated the idea of him feeling bad on her behalf. She didn't deserve his pity.

"Hey, it wasn't so bad," she said eventually, turning her body toward him and forcing herself to relax, her head coming to rest against the curve of the headrest as she lifted her gaze to his. Her intention had been to reassure him head-on that she was fine, not to ogle him at close quarters, but it was no use, a tension of a very different kind started to take over her body, clouding her mind and making it difficult to form the words she wanted to say. "I…I actually enjoyed it…for the most part."

He grinned and she felt the heat of it right down to her toes. Even in the dark, he hadn't lost his magnetism, if anything, the feeling of intimacy it created within the car only compounded it. The subtle glow from the house fell across the lower half of his face, highlighting the appealing curve to his mouth, the perfect cut to his jaw, and the teasingly open collar of his black shirt. It left the rest of him in tantalizing shadow, save for the glint in his eye, the devilish spark that made clear he was watching her and liked what he saw.

She could feel her inhibitions evaporating as her carnal instincts took over, the guilt being pushed out as the darkness engulfed them, shutting off the rest of the world and its moral compass. She looked to his mouth, not two feet away, and remembered how expertly it could work her own, coaxing responses out of her that she hadn't known possible, evoking demands from her mouth that she hadn't thought capable of uttering.

Her eyes fell to his hand resting between them, his long, confident fingers splayed across his thigh, and she remembered how masterfully they had played her, bringing her to a climax so powerful she wanted to relive it again and again.

"I can read you, Carrie."

His words rippled through her, their low, dangerous quality exciting the hairs at the back of her neck as she dared to meet his eye once more.

She licked her lips to rid their sudden dryness and heard his breath catch, his hand coming up to cup her chin.

"Are you as wet down there for me as you are up here?" he asked, brushing his thumb across her dampened mouth.

She closed her eyes and parted her lips, teasing her tongue out to meet with the underside of his thumb, the move instinctive and erotically charged.

"I bet you are," he rasped, his moistened thumb now dragging downward, creating a damp trail as it moved over her lower lip, her chin, her jaw...

Reaching her neck, he fanned his hand out to stroke his thumb and fingers on either side of her neck, the move tormentingly soft against the sensitive skin and drawing a small moan from her lips.

"Shall I see for myself?" he asked as his hand met with the fabric of her T-shirt.

He wouldn't dare, not here, not now.

But he would; his hand showed no sign of stopping. The realization had her nipples pressing through the flimsy lace of her bra in anticipation, their titivated peaks desperate for the contact. And he didn't disappoint, his caress slowing marginally, he let his thumb and forefinger brush against them in unison, making her shudder and whimper with delight.

"So willing and so ready for me, aren't you?" he said, his voice getting nearer, his hand skimming lower still as it reached her abdomen.

She sucked in a shallow breath, her tummy drawing in as she feasted on his touch.

"Open your legs for me, baby."

Her eyes snapped open at his request. She couldn't. She wouldn't. Not here…

He was leaning into her, his darkened gaze penetrating her own, seducing her with his projected desire. She felt her legs betray her, their lengths spreading beneath the encouragement of his hand. His fingers slipping between them to gently probe her sweet spot through the taut fabric of her jeans.

She moaned in abandon, the ache in her belly spreading like wildfire. He was going to tip her over the edge, right here, in front of his mother's home.

"*God, yes!*" she breathed, her hands lowering to grip the seat edge, her head lolling back against the headrest as she started to let herself go.

But then she froze as a sudden shift in light invaded the car and Bradley cursed. Ahead of them, house lights came off and on, and focusing through the haze of desire she could make out movement in the windows.

Taking his hand away, Bradley thrust it through his hair, his features tight with unrestrained need. She hadn't been the only one about to lose her cool. He'd been coming right along with her. The thought was enough to ease the burn of shame that started to creep in.

"If I don't drive, my mother is going to have something far more X-rated to take issue with," he ground out. Then, looking to her as if she didn't really have a choice, he added, "My house?"

It was all she could do to nod as the engine roared to life. She just hoped he didn't live far away. She didn't want the time to change her mind, for her conscience to take over. This was what she had intended to do all along, after all: to say to hell with her sister and enjoy herself to the fullest, or rather, enjoy Bradley to the fullest.

But it was one thing to say "to hell with it!" mentally and fantasize about all the crazy things she wanted to do with the man himself. Actually going through with it was something else entirely.

CHAPTER SIX

THE TEN-MINUTE JOURNEY TO his pad felt like an eternity.

He knew she wanted him, desire emanated around her like an aura. But he couldn't rid the feeling that he was on borrowed time, he sensed at any moment she would turn tail and beg him to take her home.

He would have blamed it on their company that evening, well, his mother to be more precise, if it hadn't been for her peculiar behavior throughout the day. It had to be the proposal hanging between them, what else could it be? He needed to confront her, clear the air and get it dealt with so that they could move forward. But he couldn't give it the concentration it deserved. Not when her coy smile was enough to make his dick hard. There wasn't a hope in hell he would make it through a serious conversation once they were alone.

He accelerated up the driveway to his hillside home, faster than he should. It was a good job he could do the journey in his sleep. The entrance to the underground garage opened as they approached and he dropped his speed, the engine purring with a teasing energy that belied the power beneath his feet. As they rolled through the entrance, he tapped the gas to get them to the end of the vast room. The roar of the engine echoed around, vibrating through them, mirroring his burning need. He maneuvered the vehicle to its pride of place at the head of the line-up and cut the engine. Triggering the doors to open, he practically leapt from the car and strode around to help Carrie out.

She slotted her hand into his outstretched palm, her eyes looking up at him beneath her lashes as she rose. And bam! There it was—that smile! His cock did a leap for joy, his brain all but vanished.

Just get to the bedroom first!

He pulled her along, her body coming willingly, her eyes scanning the entire room under her lashes. Was she looking for a way out?

"You okay?" he asked, one foot poised on the steps that led the way to the living space above. *Please, please, please say you're okay…*

Her gaze shot to his, her cheeks flushed, her eyes wide and bright, and she nodded; a surreptitious up and down movement of her head, but a nod all the same. It was enough for him! The last time they had been here, they'd returned from a red-carpet event and she had been the one in charge, the one calling all the shots. Now, she couldn't look or be more different. Clothed in her basics, her angelic appearance as she eyed him, followed him, deferred to him, gave every indication that she was his to do with as he pleased.

A surge of emotion ripped through him and he pulled her against him, crushing her lips with the ferocity of his own. His tongue invading the sweet sanctity of her mouth as she parted for him on an explosive breath, her perfectly smooth teeth grazing his lip as she shifted beneath him and granted his tongue space to play, to explore.

He growled deep in his throat, spinning her round so her back was to the stairs and perfectly positioned to take her body as he encouraged her down. She arched up to him, her bottom fitting neatly into a step as he lowered himself above her, one hand working to take his weight, the other slipping beneath the hem of her T-shirt.

He sipped at her lip, licking and tasting, intoxicated by the whimpers he was coaxing out of her.

"You have never been more beautiful," he whispered against her as his hand found one illicitly-laced mound, the hardened pearl at its center pressing into his palm. He flicked his finger over it teasingly and she cried out beneath him, her body writhing.

"You like that?" he said, his thumb and forefinger taking hold of the nub and rolling it, enticing it further.

"Yes!" she panted, her hands clutching his back, her fingers biting into his skin.

Propping his knee on the step, he extracted his hand to take hold of the hem of her top, breaking their kiss long enough to pull it over her head. Her blonde hair came tumbling in waves about her shoulders, over the white lace of her bra, the purity of both hair and fabric a direct contrast to the wanton desire burning in her gaze.

He kissed her again, his hands sliding to the fastening of her bra, unhooking it in seconds. He took her arms from around him, placing them on either side of her on the step as he teased the straps down, his hands caressing the soft, bare skin as he went.

Tossing the bra away, he pulled back, desperate to engrave the memory of how she looked right now in his mind, strewn across his steps.

Never before would she have let them do this. Not here, not on the surface of his garage stairs. Perhaps two weeks apart had cast off her idealistic tendencies in the sack.

"Come back!" she pleaded, her blue eyes dark with need, her hair falling across her breasts as her exquisite rosy-pink, upturned nubs peaked through, screaming to be sucked and teased, flicked, and groped.

His gaze dropped to her waist, her deliciously petite belly button, down to the flare of her hips as her naked flesh met with the blue of her jeans. He needed the rest. He needed the whole of her exposed to his hungry gaze. He dipped to take off her sneakers, one hand caressing her thigh while the other did the removing.

Placing the footwear aside, he straightened to take hold of the button on the fly of her jeans and popped it open. Next came the zip. He was rewarded with a flash of white briefs sporting small pink roses. They were pretty and innocent, very un-Carrie. He didn't care, he liked this new Carrie. Perhaps a little too much.

Taking hold of the waistband, he tugged them off and her legs moved willingly, her body like liquid under his attention. He threw them to join her sneakers, his eyes now lost to the sight before him. Her seductively long legs outstretched upon the steps, her upper body raised on her elbows, her eyes watching him, waiting, drawing him back as the animal in him let loose. He feasted on her mouth, her neck, her breasts, milking delicious sounds from her throat. She was twisting beneath him, her pelvis thrusting toward him as he lowered himself to press against her, his cock already at the brink as she started to ride against him. The realization that he wasn't going to last a second once he was inside her had him pulling back; he needed to make sure she was right there with him.

She whimpered. "Don't go," she pleaded, lifting herself against him and making his cock react in kind.

"Patience," he managed to say, backing his lower body away as his hand slipped between them to slide beneath the fabric of her underwear.

Christ, she was so wet! He had to grit his teeth to keep control, his eyes fixed on hers as he slid between her folds, seeking her out.

Teasingly, he circled the area, his breathing matching the out of control rate of hers.

"You want me here?" he asked, continuing the caress, taunting her with its proximity to her swollen clit.

"Yes!" she cried, shifting her hips beneath him, desperate to maneuver him where she wanted him.

"No, you don't!" He moved to kneel on either side of one leg, pinning it in place. His free hand forcing her thighs apart and steady. She whimpered and tried to move against him, but he refused to let up, forcing her to succumb to his will. She wilted beneath him, her hands falling to her sides to grip at the edge of the step.

"That's better," he said, rewarding her by circling his thumb directly over her clit.

A moan tore from her throat and he smiled down at her, loving how she threw her head back with the sound, her legs trembling at his touch. He picked up his tempo, his other hand leaving her thigh to seek out the sweet haven of her pussy, desperate to feel his fingers buried inside her.

He tested her opening, one finger, then two, slipping them into her inviting wetness. She was slick, warm, and enticingly tight, and she had his control slipping by the wayside all over again.

"More, more..." she panted, thrashing beneath him.

Sure thing, baby! He slipped in a third and she contracted around him, the wild tempo of her body encouraging him deeper and deeper as he sensed her orgasm begin to take hold.

He couldn't wait any longer. Keeping his fingers inside her, he slid his thumb upward to take over the pressure at her clit and freed his other hand to rip open his jeans.

His cock leapt free, rock solid and ready. He slid his hand over himself, his thighs tensing with the move, pre-cum seeping from the tip. He was in danger of blowing his load all over her...

"*Please, now,*" she begged, reaching around to claw at his ass in desperation.

"Fuck!" He could hardly think straight. Withdrawing his hand, he slipped her panties aside and guided his cock right over her entrance.

There was split second where he pondered the lack of protection, it was something they had always used, but the time for sanity was lost. The idea of a baby warming his core, he thrust himself inside her, possessively hard and deep.

She cried out, her body shuddering with her release. Her climax creating a suffocating assault around his plunging cock and taking him with her, the force and multitude of spasms leaving him feeling raw and winded.

His hands fell forward to either side of her as he fought to keep his sated weight from crushing her, his head bowed so that he could watch her come to beneath him. She was startlingly beautiful, her post-romp glow leaving him feeling inexplicably proud, her almost sheepish eyes glittering in the bright light of the garage, her blonde hair fanned out disorderly around her, framing her exquisitely coy little face.

"If only I had a camera right now," he said, dropping a kiss to her swollen lip. "You are truly stunning."

She made a small sound and smiled, her body shifting against the hard surface of the step and bringing him to his senses as he realized how uncomfortable she must be.

"Here, let's get you off these stairs," he said grabbing up her discarded T-shirt and offering it to her as he moved to stand.

She stood with him and pulled the top over her head, her flushed body still distractingly appealing, even in his sated state. He wasn't ready for the evening to be over, not yet. He wanted to enjoy her company well into the night.

"I'm starving, you hungry?" he said, putting himself back into his pants and scooping up the remainder of her clothing.

"Hungry?" she asked dumbly.

"You know, food?" he teased, as he took hold of her hand to lead her up the stairs.

"Sounds good," she said softly. "I could just do with freshening up first."

"Sure thing."

He pushed open the door at the top of the stairs. He didn't turn the lights on immediately. It was a habit, he liked to make the most of the glass-walled view over Hollywood that welcomed him home. It never ceased to relax him, the ability to watch down over Tinseltown in all its buzzing glory and remain detached; it was a metaphor for how he lived his life.

"Wow!"

The sound came from Carrie behind him as she stilled in the doorway, her eyes drinking in the far-reaching view. He couldn't remember her reacting like this before, but then he figured they hadn't just had sex in the garage before either.

"I know," he said tossing his keys on the side. "I'm still not used to it and I've been living here for years."

He pushed open the door that led to the nearest restroom and planted a kiss against her hair. "Off you go, I'll see you in the kitchen."

She walked around him, her hand trailing in his own right up until the point she entered the doorway. Giving him the smile he was fast falling for, she said, "I won't be long."

It wasn't until the door clicked shut that his brain kicked back in and he remembered the remainder of her clothing was still tucked under his arm. He went to tap on the door but stopped himself, smiling as he headed instead for the kitchen—it wouldn't hurt to keep her in just T-shirt and undies for a little while longer…

What the hell had she just done?

She glared at her reflection in the mirror. The question was becoming all too frequent now that Bradley was in her life, she realized, taking in her tortured expression. It was an accurate depiction of the raging battle letting rip inside her head. How could she have been so stupid? Having sex with him had been her bold intention, of course, but to have done it without any protection was plain foolish. Where was her common sense? Evidently, she'd left it behind in the UK, along with the male-immune version of herself. But in truth, it hadn't even entered her head as she'd pleaded with him to be inside her. It was only with the clarity that came from locking herself in the bathroom, out of his mind-disabling presence, that she had twigged.

And it also wasn't lost on her that a lack of condom hadn't bothered Bradley. Obviously, Carrie must have birth control covered.

But she didn't. It had never been a concern.

Bloody idiot!

There was nothing else for it but to get to a pharmacy as soon as she could tomorrow and get whatever it was she needed. She could make up some excuse to Amy and disappear briefly. That's if there was a pharmacy she could use…

Of course there would be, she told herself, pushing back the rising panic.

But first, she needed to get through the night. Would he take her home after food or would he expect her to stay? Should she ask him to take her home? It must be pushing ten thirty. It hardly seemed fair to expect him to drive her.

At least he wouldn't want to have sex again, men needed time to recover after all. Or so she believed. Disappointment washed over her unchecked. Oh God, *her* body clearly didn't need any time to recover!

She had wanted him…no, still wanted him, with a need so powerful it terrified her. The desire he had built within her had all but consumed her, evaporating every thought, every doubt, until all that had been left was the need to have him.

There had been no room for sanity, no checking for protection, no guilt, nothing. Just pure, exhilarating passion. Even now, her cheeks were filled with the heat of it, her brain on fire with the memory.

She knew she would have to admit the act to Carrie again, she was too honest for her own good. It was just as well that this was all Carrie's fault at the end of the day. It really, really was.

But then she thought of Bradley and her guilt soared, her tummy twisting with the sickening realization of what she was doing to him: deceiving him, letting him think she was someone else and having him open up to her in the most intimate ways possible. She clutched her hand to her mouth, her eyes clamping shut.

What was it Carrie had said? "He won't like the falsity of it"? One thing was certain, he would hate them for it. And the very idea of someone like Bradley hating her, all but crippled her.

She let it sink in, her mind playing out the various scenarios of what she could possibly do to make the situation right again and only one came with a tolerable conclusion. Whatever happened, she had to ensure that he never worked out who she was. She needed to give the performance of a lifetime and see it out until her sister could get herself back. Carrie could then take over her life once more, Bradley would be none the wiser and Isla could get her arse home, never to be in this position again.

It was a sound plan. So, why did it leave her feeling so utterly crap inside?

But then, something even worse struck her: what if Carrie came back and decided not to break it off with Bradley? What if she actually married him?

Nausea almost floored her. Carrie wouldn't dare, surely? Not when she'd had to fly across the Atlantic to flee the proposal in the first place.

A tap at the door made her jump and she stared at it in open horror, unable to face him just yet.

"You fancy waffles, babe?"

Even his voice, muffled through the door, made her insides quiver with reignited excitement. What the hell was wrong with her? Not a second before, she had been sick with worry and what could only be described as a fierce jealousy. Now, she just wanted to jump his bones anew.

I'm going to Hell in a hand basket!

"Waffles would be great," she squeaked back, wincing at the harried state of her voice and forcing out "thanks" at a much more normal tone.

Turning on the cold tap, she thrust her palms under the flow and splashed it over face, dousing it as best she could before taking up the hand towel and patting herself dry. Stepping back, she critically assessed her reflection: her skin glowed, her eyes sparkled, her lips were all puffy, and her hair was wild, she emanated a vibrancy that was totally new on her. And he was the cause, he had done all this "crazy" to her and she should be miffed with herself, not loving it.

She lowered her gaze to the two peaks, braless and still hard against the fabric of her tee, a screaming visual of the desire burning through her veins. It was no use fighting or denying it, she was putty where he was concerned. And it would be far simpler if, for the time she had left with him, she shut off her moral code and gave her innate feelings free reign. She wasn't naive, she knew full well that if she properly set her mind to it, she could make her two legs walk the way of his front door and leave. But she was being greedy. She wanted the crazy passion he inspired in her. And for as long as time permitted, she would take all she could get. After all, if she was going to Hell, she might as well enjoy the ride.

Ignoring her judgmental reflection, she took hold of the door handle and swung it open. Brazenly stepping out before her nerves could resurface, she headed toward the glass-walled view, the sounds emanating from the area telling her she was on track for the kitchen.

She found him, all sexy and domesticated, beating a batter into submission behind an enormous white breakfast bar.

"There you are," he said, looking up from the bowl.

She wanted to whimper just at the sight of him, any moment she expected a director to announce action and have him toss the bowl aside so he could take her up and screw her over the counter, like in some domestic fantasy flick. She tried to give him a normal smile in return and worried she looked deranged. Thankfully, he turned his attention back to the mix and freed her to survey the room.

It was an incredible place. To her right was the living area with its gray plush sofas, cream leather wing chair, and the blue-lit swimming pool beyond the glass. Straight ahead sat an enormous natural wood dining table with at least ten red funky chairs lining it. The horizon that was Hollywood by night, stretched out beyond. And to her left was the kitchen, the size of which put her commercial kitchen at the club to shame.

She couldn't shake the feeling that she was on a film set, it was just too surreal. If not a director, then she expected a tour guide to pop up and show her round. It reminded her of the Stahl House Carrie had once sent her pictures of, back when she was seventeen and doing the tourist thing.

But, reality check, she was no tourist right now, and the guy to her left, acting surprisingly homely and making his own waffles—*from scratch!*—was certainly no guide.

"You afraid if you come any nearer I might jump you?" he said, his brows raised quizzically as he took in her unmoving form on the threshold.

"Sorry, just taking it all in," she said, giving a nonchalant shrug that she certainly didn't feel and adding the word "again" before he thought the remark odd.

"I was getting worried you had flushed yourself away," he joked, as she forced one leg in front of the other and approached him.

"Do you have my clothes somewhere?"

"I've put them in the bedroom." He paused to give her a mischievous grin. "I figure you don't need them right now."

"Oh, I see," she said, fighting a creeping blush as she took up one of the black leather stools positioned at the bar.

Propping her elbows on the surface, her head in her hands, she watched him, her hungry eyes devouring every inch. He'd unbuttoned his shirt midway down his chest (or had she done that back in the garage?) and his sleeves were rolled back to his elbows, the muscles in his bronzed forearms flexing with his effort to work the batter. His hair fell forward across his forehead as he now gave the mix his full attention.

Breathtakingly handsome didn't even cut it.

How could her sister not have been marching this man down the aisle? What was it Isla was missing?

"Do you do this often?" she asked, nodding to the bowl in his hands and then regretting her blunder almost immediately; Carrie would know the answer to this already, surely?

He gave her a cheeky smile. "Not when you've been here. I've never felt you would appreciate waffles being served up so close to bed, but after that session, I figured I might be able to coax you with one."

Excitement trickled through her at the images his reference to their "session" painted in her mind.

"Sounds perfect," she said, and meant it. Comfort eating was one of her many vices and right now her stress levels were demanding a truckload of carbs.

His eyes narrowed on her. "That sounds like a hungry 'perfect'." He turned to pour the batter into the awaiting waffle pan. "Think I'd best make more."

"Can I help?"

She didn't like to be idle. Especially when she couldn't trust herself not to physically drool over his working form and the motion of his hands that had worked her so masterfully.

"Sure, you fancy some wine?" he asked, nodding to a cabinet at the end of the light wooden units lining the wall behind him.

"Wine and waffles, my idea of heaven," she said, slipping off the bar stool and sauntering past him, her body prickling with awareness as he watched her every step.

"You choose," he said as she paused before the glass door, unveiling a vast array of bottles.

Where did she even start? Luckily, this was an area she knew something about.

"You like your wine," she said approvingly.

"Hmm, I like you more," he slipped in there, his eyes raking over her at length and drawing out a smile from beneath her lashes.

"Could you be any more smooth?" she asked, giving him a teasing shake of her head. "We won't have any waffles if you keep getting distracted."

He chuckled and turned away, his attention dutifully returning to his batter-making.

His back was now to her, but she was no less drawn in, her body being pulled by an invisible force to go to him, to slip her arms around him and enjoy him while he worked. Would he like her to do that? Would Carrie do that?

She swallowed down her mental ramblings and tried to concentrate on her own task, opening the cabinet door and scanning the collection. She brushed her fingers over the many bottle heads, feeling a comforting sense of familiarity.

Extracting a bottle here and there, she could see he had exceptional taste, but then she would expect nothing less. She hummed as she contemplated her preference, her mind now solely on the perfect pairing and coming up blank. She needed a long drink. Not a Muscat or other such wine that normally accompanied a sweet dish, and Champagne felt too much like celebrating.

She bent forward at the hip, her eyes seeking out a sparkling white that didn't break the bank.

"If you want this batter to remain in the bowl I suggest you hurry up and grab something, your sweet behind is not helping me remain focused."

Her cheeks flushed as she sent him a look over her shoulder. His eyes were intent on her exposed bottom, desire etched in his taut expression, the bowl tilted in his slackened hold. She looked away quickly, doing her best to calm the rising heat within.

"You're insatiable," she accused, her mind dealing with the realization that perhaps men don't need too long to recover, after all.

Subconsciously, she pulled at the back of her T-shirt, stretching it over her bottom as she plucked out a bottle.

She heard him chuckle and she spun on her heel, her eyebrows raised in question. "What's so funny?"

"Nothing," he said, his eyes dancing.

So, he found her amusing, did he? Peeling the foil away from the bottle, she held his gaze, his humor rubbing off on her and making her brazen.

"You know, you should never provoke someone holding fizz," she warned, shaking up the bottle in her hands.

He eyed her. "Is that so?"

"Oh, yes, it is a very silly move," she said deliberately slow, her hands working to untwist the metal that held the cork secure.

"You wouldn't dare," he said, his gaze dropping to the bottle and then back to her face.

It was the wrong thing to say.

Tossing the wire to the side, she pushed the cork off, sending it with an explosive pop across the room. Pressing her thumb over the opening, she forced the fizz into a fountain and aimed it straight at him, showering him from head to foot.

She couldn't help the laugh that erupted, or the warmth in her core as his soaked clothing sucked into his muscular form like a second skin.

But then he moved, the batter tossed to the side as he flicked his wet hair back and strode toward her. "You're in so much trouble."

She squealed, her laugh becoming one of nervous excitement as she tried to evade him, dodging his arms as he swung to grab her and dashing to put the counter between them.

"You deserved it," she accused, placing the bottle on the surface, her knees bent and body poised to counteract his next step.

"Really?" he said, taking a step toward her, his eyes flashing dangerously.

She nodded.

He leapt across the surface of the breakfast bar, a move she had only witnessed in movies, and was upon her before she could even contemplate which way to go.

"Got you," he said chuckling at her startled expression as he gripped her in his arms. "And now, it's payback."

She looked up at him, her body alive with the damp pressure of his as he reached out to take hold of the bottle.

"You really wouldn't dare..." she said cying the bottle as he maneuvered it above her head, her giggles now stifled with disbelief and the sexual undercurrent that was positively buzzing between them.

He raised his brows. "Wouldn't I?"

She just had chance to close her eyes before the liquid poured over her, flowing over her open mouth, down her chin, over her T-shirt, and pooling on the floor at their feet.

She swallowed the drink that had made it into her mouth, and panted. "It's good."

"You want more?"

"There can't be much left."

"There's enough," he said, teasing her chin upward with one hand, while the other poured the liquid with perfect aim down her throat, his eyes turning dark as he watched her swallow.

"Save me some," he commanded, tipping more into her mouth before closing it off with his own, his tongue lapping inside her, teasing the liquid out of her mouth and into his own. "I have to say it tastes better when it comes off you."

"Ditto," she whispered, her tongue flicking out to lick her lips, her uneven breathing matching the race of her heart. She was about to say "more" when a sudden smell hit her, causing her noise to wrinkle. "Do you smell burning?"

"Damn it!" he cursed, swiftly releasing her and slipping over the damp floor to get to the waffle machine that was currently smoking.

"I can devour waffles, burnt or not," she assured him, giggling as he extracted two blackened squares.

"No chance," he said, tossing them into the bin and taking up the bowl. "Don't worry, I have enough to produce a fleet of waffles, just you wait."

"You might want to change before you stick the next lot on?" she suggested, her eyes scanning his damp clothing and her mouth going dry, despite the recent drink.

"I have a better idea," he said, pouring the next lot in regardless. "I'm thinking—waffles, wine, and bath."

"Bath?" she repeated. *Together?* her mind mentally added, her pulse racing at the prospect.

"Yes," he confirmed, his burning gaze back on her. "I'm not the only one in need of a change."

She looked down at her tee, the fabric was now flesh-colored where the liquid had hit and clung against her. "Point taken."

"Come on," he said gruffly, offering her his hand.

She gladly took it, her eyes flicking to the waffle pan and back to him.

"What about the waffles?"

"I will come back to those once I have you settled in the bathroom."

As he passed the wine cabinet, he pulled out a fresh bottle and hooked up a glass with his finger.

"Are you not having a bath?" she asked, noting the single glass and trying not to sound disappointed as she followed him.

"Oh, don't worry, I'll join you just as soon as they're made." He glanced back at her, and the heat in his eye had Isla swallowing down an excited whimper.

Recovery time? As if!

CHAPTER SEVEN

CARRIE COULDN'T HAVE BEEN MORE hidden if she had still been clothed.

Since when did a grown woman need a bath overflowing with bubbles? And not just a thin layer of fluff, she had created great, big, billowing clouds of the stuff. There was no way they would be able to eat waffles. Not unless they fancied the things à la soap!

"You sure you got enough bubbles in there?" he said, kicking the door to the bathroom closed as he made his way to the sunken bathtub at the heart of the room, a tray of waffles, strawberries, and wine glasses in his outstretched hands.

Carrie peeked over the fluff. "I think I may have made a mistake putting the jets on," she said apologetically, her damp face flushing as she hurried to clear the bubbles from the side of the tub to make space for the tray. "I turned them off but the damage was already done."

A strange warmth encircled his chest at the sight of her, all humble and adorable and so very unlike her. It wasn't desire, it wasn't need, it was something new and unsettling. Trying to ignore the intrusive thought, he crouched to set the tray down, his body immediately coming alive at the proximity of her naked form, bubbles or no.

"I can honestly say I've not experienced a bubble bath in all my adult years," he said, as he straightened and began to peel off his clothing. "So, this will be a new one for me."

He watched her eyes widen with each discarded item of clothing, her expression one of obvious appreciation and he would have reveled in it, if not for the nervous undercurrent also buzzing off her.

"You okay?" he asked.

"Uh-huh," she piped, her gaze lifting momentarily to his before she disappeared under the water, the bubbles parting and then converging above her.

What the devil?

He shrugged off his clothing and moved to the opposite end of the bath. With trepidation, he stepped into the water, easing in gently so as to avoid the possibility of stepping on her. Where the bloody hell was she?

Just as he thought it, she appeared, her bubble-covered head emerging from the water on an exhale that sent tufts of white gliding through the air.

"This bath is huge," she said, rubbing her eyes to rid them of soap, her face relaxing as he submerged his entire body into the water, his legs making tantalizing contact with her own.

"It's not the only thing," he said, the throb of his body upping in severity as the need to feel her naked against him overruled every other thought. "Come here."

She swallowed. "Where?"

He reached out to catch her wrist and pulled her toward him.

She moved slowly, her body gliding through the water, caressing his own as she slid along. He dropped his hands to her hips and turned her, positioning her curvaceous bottom between his legs. He couldn't prevent the buck of his cock against her and sensed her stiffen at the contact.

"I'm afraid my body is having a tough time staying in control where your naked self is concerned."

She gave a shaky breath. "It's not the only one."

"That's good to hear," he murmured into her ear, his hands coming up to caress her arms.

He could feel the tension running through her, and he wanted it gone, pronto.

"Thirsty?" he asked.

She nodded against him and he reached out for the bottle, his other hand taking up a caress over her arm as he did so, his fingers trailing with teasing softness from the top of her shoulder to her wrist and back again. She sighed into him and he smiled to himself, he would have her relaxed in no time.

Setting the bottle down, he took up the glass and offered it to her.

"Thank you," she said, her hand slipping around his, her delicate touch making his body thrum with all the things he wanted those hands to do.

"You're welcome," he managed to get out.

Fearing that his overeager cock was going to unsettle her anew, he tried to distract himself by pouring a second glass, but Carrie stopped him.

"We can share," she said, turning her head toward him and offering up her own glass.

Share?

Had he really just heard her correctly? The Carrie he knew always insisted on her own glass, her own cutlery, her own plate, her own everything. His heart tightened. What was she about?

He was about to take the glass from her but changed his mind. Encouraging the closeness he could feel growing between them, he brought his head alongside her and offered up his mouth for her to pour into. She smiled and did as he wished, her eyes watching him under her lashes, her lower lip caught beneath her teeth in a telling manner. It was rousingly intimate and so fucking sexy…

The cold drink sparkled on his tongue, the sensation a delicious contrast to the heat in his loins, and the temperature of the bathwater. He forced out an appreciative sigh, keen not to spook her with the ferocity of his desire.

"That drink was a good choice," he said, his head straightening to allow his hands to take up position on either side of her neck, his thumb and fingers working against the tension in her shoulders.

She gave a small moan of delight, her body shuffling against him in open encouragement. He deepened the massage, his fingers rotating over her with growing confidence as she relaxed further and further into him. Her head dropping forward to grant him better access to her neck.

"Why are you so tense?" he asked, the question was out before he could think better of it. Was he really ready for the discussion he knew they needed to have?

"Hmm," she said, her head lolling with his movement.

"To be honest, you've seemed off since I returned."

"Have I?"

He knew he had hit a nerve; her voice was high and he could feel the tension mounting once more beneath his fingers.

"Look, we have to talk about this at some point, Carrie," he persisted, keen to get the conversation out of the way. "Was it how I proposed?"

She turned to stone beneath him.

"How you proposed?" she repeated, moving to take a large swig of the wine still in her hand. If she hadn't been in the bath with him, he had a feeling she would have run away rather than furthered the discussion.

"Yes," he said, his hands kneading her skin, unrelenting in their quest to have her chill out. "It was never my intention to change our relationship as such. It just felt like a natural progression. You know my feelings on love…well, our feelings, really. We've often said it's for the weak and misguided."

She flinched.

"Sorry, did I hurt you?" he asked, concerned that he had caught her shoulder badly.

"No, you're fine," she said quietly. "Go on."

He softened his caress all the same. "Trust is what you and I are about, Carrie."

He lowered his lips to nuzzle at her neck.

"Trust and incredible sex," he whispered against her, feeling her shiver beneath him.

"We're good company for one another, it takes away the loneliness, gives you an excuse to turn away the men that won't take no as an answer"—she snorted softly at that—"and drive you crazy for all the wrong reasons. You know it makes sense."

Silence. She sipped at her drink. Once. Twice.

Desperation kicked in. He wanted, no, *needed* her to cave, to hear the word "yes" leave her lips.

"Come on, Carrie, our lifestyles are perfectly suited," he stressed. "Our attitudes are totally aligned and, above all, we know it's a fantastic publicity move for you."

She froze. He felt every bit of her chill under the last.

"Publicity?" she said icily.

"Well, yes. Not that you need it," he assured her. "You don't need anyone to boost your career, babe."

He was losing her, it was blatantly obvious. But why? The mention of publicity should have sealed the deal not tipped her over the edge. After all, her priority when they had started dating had been to be seen together. They had openly agreed it was a good thing for her career. She had orchestrated many a social gathering and when the press had chosen against publicizing their relationship for other news, often more sinister, fabricated stories, he had figured the proposal to be the perfect move.

So, why should that hurt her now? And why had it also left a bitter taste in his own mouth when he had vocalized it just then? Why the change in both of them?

"Trust, sex, and a boost for my career," she said distractedly, as though slowly absorbing everything for the first time. Like they hadn't had this conversation just over two weeks ago.

Suddenly, she turned into him, her knees coming up to rest either side of his hips, the water sloshing around them with the speed of her move.

"And what do you get out of this arrangement?" she sparked, her eyes intent on him as she issued the question, her hand depositing the now empty glass on the side and blindly replacing it with the bottle.

He was too stunned to speak, his cock coming alive at the apex of her thighs. His eyes lost to the bubbles sliding away from her upper body as they unveiled her achingly full breasts, her nipples hard and demanding, her torso toned and slick.

He swallowed. If this was some weird fighting technique to get the upper hand, he was all for it.

"There must be something in it for you?" she pushed as she raised the bottle to her open mouth and took a sip. Her tongue wrapping around her lips on the tail end of the move. Her eyes still fixed on him, their depths hot and heavy.

She knew what she was doing.

"Hmm?" She raised her brows with attitude and his dick sparked. "What does the amazing Bradley King get out of marrying Carrie Evans?"

"I get you," he growled, his hands reaching for her hips, desperate to drive into her. "I get you riding my cock, at every possible opportunity, I get you taking me in your hand just like you are that bottle, and bringing me to your mouth. Sucking *me* dry."

"Easy, tiger!" she blurted, her free hand coming down to pin against his chest, her body lifting away from his seeking cock.

He fell back and watched as she took another deep swig of the bottle, the move deliberately slow and erotic, her eyes holding his gaze in a hypnotically controlling fashion.

He groaned his surrender, even as his body shifted defiantly beneath her, and she gave him a triumphant sexy-as-fuck smile.

"Drink?" She offered the bottle up to his lips, her eyes lowering to his mouth, their depths screaming of her debauched cravings.

"Hell, yeah!" he said, pushing his chin out to accept the flow as she poured it into his awaiting mouth.

"It's my turn to taste it off you," she said thickly, her lips coming down over his, her delicate tongue easing into him as she lapped up what she could.

The move was his undoing. Taking hold of her thigh in one hand, he grabbed his throbbing shaft and before she had chance to react, he brought her down forcefully over him.

Crying out, her body arched, her breasts thrusting enticingly toward him, her head thrown back with her dampened locks while her pussy clamped tight about him. It was a sight and sensation overload, filling him with the heady telltale tension that he just wasn't ready for. Not yet!

He took hold of her hips to keep her still. "Put down the bottle."

She looked at him questioningly, her expression hazy with desire.

"Do it!" he ground out, his hands working hard to stop her moving over him. Christ, she felt so good.

Obediently, she placed the bottle on the side, her hand coming back to comb a stray lock from her face as she looked to him expectantly for more.

"Good girl," he said, his gaze dropping leisurely over her upper body, his mind racing with what he wanted next. "Now touch yourself."

Her eyes widened. "I'm not…I can't…"

He almost choked on his own need. "You can."

She hesitated, a sudden innocence emerging in her expression. "Where?"

Positioning her small hand in his, he brought her up to cup one ripe mound, his thumb brushing across the aroused nipple. She bucked against him, a moan escaping her lips.

"Feels good, doesn't it?" He squeezed, his hand tightening around her own to grope at the tender flesh, guiding her to take pleasure in her own caress. He coaxed her until he felt her take the lead, exploring her own skin, her own nipple…

He caught up her other hand, encouraging her to pay the same attention to the other breast. She needed no persuasion, the hand took to the task like a pro, both hands now working over her upper body with a hunger so fierce it had her writhing over him.

"Oh my God, that feels so good," she moaned, her hips gyrating in a long, rhythmic motion that teased him with its slowness and he had to force himself to stand down, to let her dictate the pace.

"That's it, baby, go with it." He dropped his palms to the curve of her thighs and lost himself to the illicit show she was performing. "Now rub your clit for me."

To his dark approval, she gave no hesitation this time. Slipping a hand from her breast, she slid it across her torso and through the surface of the water. Gasping as she found her spot and began to ride both his cock and her own fingers in unison. Her other hand continuing to pinch and grope at her breast with punishing delight. Desperately, he tried to burn the sight into his memory banks, battling with the swell of tension that was threatening to take hold.

"Yes!" she cried out above him, the water slapping noisily as her tempo became fierce and out-of-control.

He couldn't take anymore, his willpower in tatters, he grabbed her hips and pumped her over him at a frenzied rate, sending them both into an earth-shattering fuck that there was no coming back from.

He exploded into her, his entire being buzzing with the exhilarating release. She followed, hot on his tail, her body thrashing as her climax ripped through her.

Water sloshed around them in undulating waves that escaped the bathtub. He didn't care. It was worth every bit of the mess.

It was a while before the tremors passed, for both of them, but as soon as he was able, he raised his arms to pull her down, eager to have her against him again.

She came willingly, nestling her head beneath his chin, her head well above water level now that the bubbles and much of the bath had emptied out onto the bathroom floor.

"I think we've ruined another batch of waffles," she said eventually.

Her words drove a relieved chuckle from his bones.

Thank God, all is good again!

"Ruined waffles I can live with," he said. "A ruined you and I, I can't."

CHAPTER EIGHT

ISLA WOKE TO AN EMPTY bed. Her body aching head to toe from the night's activities.

They had moved from the bath, to the kitchen, to the sofa, to the bed, each surface being treated to a thorough pounding of their bodies. Once she had let go, there was no going back and no matter how many times she came, she still couldn't get enough of him. Not when he looked at her like he did. It was unbelievably insane, the stuff of dreams, to have the fantasy of her formative years look at her like she was the most desirable woman he had ever set eyes on. It was no wonder she had surrendered her entire moral code to be with him.

Heat crept into her cheeks as she remembered the things they had done. What she had let him do. What she had, in turn, done to him.

She'd wiped out her ten years of abstinence in one crazy, unrelenting night.

She peeped through her heavy lids. Sunlight streaked between the blinds into the white room. The space where he had slept lay rumpled and empty before her. She reached out, her hand tracing the path where his body had lain, the soft gray sheets still warm to her touch.

Where had he gone? And what time was it? They had promised Amy they would collect her at nine thirty and she still needed to get home for some clothes.

The smell of coffee reached her nostrils, its heady, arousing scent a godsend.

Pulling the top sheet around her, she crawled off the bed and padded out of the room.

She found him in the kitchen. This time shirtless, a pair of tight-fitting black trunks the only thing protecting his modesty.

"Hey, sleepyhead," he said, looking up as she approached, the warmth in his eyes enough to take her breath away. "I was about to bring you breakfast."

She stifled a yawn and hugged the sheet closer to her chest, suddenly feeling decidedly out of place in the grandness of the kitchen and in his supreme naked presence. Why hadn't she thought to check her appearance before she had left the room? Or at the very least, tried to deal with her morning breath!

"That's very kind of you," she said, surreptitiously trying to assess her breath while scanning the room for a reflection of any sort. "What time is it?"

"Eight-thirty."

Her gaze shot to him in horror. They were going to be late!

"Don't worry," he assured her, spying her worry. "I've messaged Amy and told her we'll be a little late, it's no trouble for her."

"But what about your work?"

He smiled, striding over to her, his hands parting the sheet enough to slip his arms about her bare waist, his touch sending well-rehearsed sparks through her and obliterating her self-conscious woes.

"Work can wait, this is far more enjoyable"—he kissed her forehead—"far more precious"—he kissed the tip of her nose—"far more time-worthy." He finished with his teeth nibbling at her lower lip, a low rumble kick-starting in his throat. "And if I don't step away from you this second I'm going to ruin another load of waffles."

"Did you say waffles?" she whispered leaning back, her eyes fixed on his lips as she tried to control her hunger for him, despite the growl of her tummy at the mention of food.

"I did, I figured I owed you an untainted batch." He set her away from him and gestured to the plates she hadn't seen previously. "*Et voilà*! Waffles round two...or should that be three?"

Two plates stacked high with an added side of fruit sat on the worktop, begging to be devoured.

"They look delish!" she said, her tummy rumbling in greater protest now that food was in sight.

He chuckled. "You sound more British than ever. Is that what excitement does for you or are you trying out some extreme method acting for a new part?"

"You could say that," she said, realizing how close to the mark he was.

"I like it...now sit," he ordered gesturing to the table. "It's time to replenish your energy levels after last night's antics."

Heat soared to her cheeks at his blatant reference to their exertions and her lack of clothing nagged at her.

"But I'm naked," she protested. She also smelled of sex. In fact, she could already feel herself responding to his touch from seconds before in the most telling way, her nakedness making it all the more evident.

"And?" he said, his eyebrows raised, daring her to tell him it was unacceptable. "That's how I like you."

He scooped up the plates and headed to the table, clearly unfazed by his own scant attire that too revealed just how close he was to binning his third batch of waffles and taking her back to bed. She gulped and tore her gaze away before he could spy her looking.

"Sit," he insisted, setting the plates down next to one another at the table-end so that they could sit alongside the view. "I'll just get the coffee."

As he headed back into the kitchen, she used the opportunity of having his back turned to open up the sheet and wrap it beneath her arms tightly like a strapless gown before plonking herself down.

He returned with a tray containing milk, sugar, mugs, and a steaming coffee pot. It smelled fantastic.

Eager, she picked up the pot and poured a mug full, moving for the milk next, their hands colliding over the carton.

"Sorry," she said, her eyes lifting to his. "You first."

His eyes narrowed as his hand fell away from the milk. "No, you go."

"Thanks," she said, lifting the carton and pouring.

"When did you start having milk in your coffee?"

Her hand floundered over the mug, the milk missing its target and splashing the surface.

"Oops, sorry," she said, moving to get a cloth.

"I've got it," he said shooting up and heading to the kitchen. "No need to spill it you know, I was just curious as to what changed your mind over dairy products?"

Oh, Christ! Carrie wasn't going through that phase again!

She shrugged. "Life's too short an' all that."

"I wished I'd known," he said smiling as he returned to the table, cloth in hand. "My waffles would have tasted so much better!"

"I bet these are amazing regardless," she said, relieved that he seemed to have taken her blunder in his stride.

Picking up her cutlery, she forked a piece of waffle and stuffed it into her awaiting mouth. It was a taste explosion, positively delicious!

"Actually, these are better than amazing," she mumbled, her mouth full of food.

He chuckled. "They must be if you can't pause long enough to speak between mouthfuls."

Her face burned, where were her manners! "Sorry."

Oh God, she did it again!

Swallowing down the food before she could embarrass herself any further with another repeat, she gave him a sheepish smile.

"Don't be, I'll take it as a compliment," he assured her, drizzling his own with syrup and offering the bottle to her. "You want some?"

She nodded, giddy as a child. "Please!"

She was in food heaven! Yes, it was only waffles, but they were damn good waffles and her foodie-self was falling for him good and proper. She pushed the flippant thought aside and took the bottle from him, overloading her stack with glee. She could feel him watching her and knew he was probably wondering yet again where his Carrie had gone, but in that precise moment she didn't care, a good comfort food sesh was just what she needed. Especially when she knew there was one thing she had to do that morning that she was dreading with a passion.

"Thank you for agreeing to help Amy today," he said, turning his attention back to his own plate. "She's really taken to you and Lord knows with a mother like ours she could do with some good female influences in her life."

Chewing another mouthful, she thought about what he was saying and wondered just how much she (or rather Carrie) was supposed to know about him and his mother. Careful to swallow first, she said, "Perhaps your mother means well, deep down."

She saw his grip tighten around his coffee mug and realized how far off the truth she was, at least in his eyes.

"There was a time I might have believed that," he said. "She wasn't always so…"

His voice trailed off and his gaze drifted to the view, his tortured blue depths tugging at her heartstrings.

She would have regretted her words, if not for the innate feeling that he needed this. He needed to talk, to let go of the troubles that sat buried beneath his suave exterior. And in that moment, she didn't feel like an imposter, she felt like a friend, someone whom he could confide in and entrust to share his burden.

She didn't push, she wasn't so crass as to make him talk if he didn't want to, but she waited patiently, toying with her food as she watched him.

"When I was born," he began eventually, his eyes returning to the table but his gaze unseeing, "my mother was just eighteen. Her and my father had been childhood sweethearts and he'd done the honorable thing and married her. They moved to LA to try and make a go of her acting career. He'd work long hours in the bars and she would rope in friends to help babysit so that she could attend acting classes, screenings, and pull in what work she could."

He paused to take hold of his coffee mug in two hands, propping his elbows on the table and sipping thoughtfully at the hot liquid.

"We had a few good years…from what I can remember, at any rate," he said, his lips quirking at the corners, the move so fleeting she wondered if she'd imagined it as he spoke again. "And everything seemed real good, her career was steady, nothing huge but enough to improve our living circumstances…and then it all changed, work started to dry up, they started to fight, I'd get caught in the middle…"

He lowered his lashes, shielding her from his expression, but it was too late, the raw pain she had caught a sight of, haunted her; her heart twisted for the poor boy that he once was and the man he had become.

"I'm so sorry," she said, her hand instinctively coming to rest against his wrist. "You don't need to tell me this."

He cleared his throat and gave her a half smile. "It's fine, it's good to talk about it on occasion, it's good to remind myself of why I don't let her get under my skin," he said. "Anyway, when I was ten, her career started to pick up again and our home life improved, it was all good. Until I came home sick from school one day. Dad and I found her shacked up with some guy from the production company where she was working." He shrugged off the words, his tale coming thick and fast now as he clearly sought to tell her without causing any more upset, for either of them. "Then everything became clear, the reason behind her resurgent career, the sudden influx in money. They had a blazing row and the rest, as they say, is history. He drank himself to an early grave and she slept her way through enough men to get to where she is now."

It didn't matter how flippant his tone was, Isla still felt the chill of his story deep in her bones and she couldn't help it as once again she found herself apologizing. "I'm so, so sorry."

"Hey, don't you worry about it, babe," he said, his voice warming as he placed his hand over Isla's and squeezed. "It's not all bad. She brought Amy into my life, after all, and although her motivation for having her was questionable, ultimately it doesn't matter."

"Questionable?" she asked aghast, unable to guess at what that meant but knowing it wouldn't be good. "How do you mean?"

"Having Amy was Marie's way of keeping hold of her third husband after he threatened her with divorce," he explained matter-of-factly.

"*Third husband?*"

"Yup." Then adding with a hint of bitterness, "That poor sap went the same way as my father."

Jesus, this is messed up!

"So, what number is she on now?" Dare she ask the question…?

"Charles is her fourth husband." He stabbed a piece of waffle but made no attempt to eat it. "Which brings us to the real reason for Amy's party. You see, Marie gives the impression that she is playing the doting mother, wanting to throw her daughter a twenty-first birthday bash, but it's really all about Charles and his desire to meet with me to go over some new film script he would like me to bankroll."

Isla's mouth opened to protest, to say that it can't possibly be the case, that no mother could be that heartless, but then everything he said washed over her and she realized, she had no place to object. He had more than enough reason to doubt his mother's motives.

"So, that is why she is doing this despite Amy's fears of a relapse?"

"Exactly."

"Oh my, that's awful!" she said, retrieving her hand to place it over her lips, her own appetite non-existent with his revelation. How could a mother be this self-absorbed and callous to her own children?

"When Amy lost her father," he continued, "I made it my mission to look out for her, to do everything in my power to make sure she doesn't go the way of our mother, to keep her on the straight and narrow…" His eyes were lost to her again as his memories took over, his words almost to himself as he added, "I nearly failed her once. I won't do it again."

"You mean when she became an addict?"

He winced at her words and she regretted them immediately. "Sorry," she said, dropping her hand to the table.

"No, you're right, that's precisely what I mean, I should have been around her more. LA isn't the best city to grow up in when you have family issues, it can be a lonely place and it's too easy to turn to the wrong people for comfort."

"Then why do *you* stay? Why live in Hollywood when it's played such a devastating role in your life? In your family's life?"

"I don't see it that way, I take pleasure in acting and creating movies, the ability to be someone else, to lose myself in film, to create a world that others can lose themselves in." His voice lifted with his words, his love of film ringing through. "It's magical. It may be make-believe, but sometimes the cold reality of life can be too much to bear and movies give you a temporary solace. They were certainly that for me when I was growing up."

"I guess that makes sense," she said slowly, taking on board what he was saying.

"Hollywood can be amazing if you see it through the right eyes. Ultimately, what can hurt you here is the same as anywhere else in the world, it's just up to us to protect ourselves from it."

She nodded.

"It's why I sensed we had such a good connection," he continued, his hand coming down to cover her own on the table top. "That night we met, we just clicked, you and your experience with your parents, me with mine, it hadn't been just the wine talking that night."

Reference to his and Carrie's first night, made her tummy slump and she wanted off the subject. "Yes, well, I still hold Hollywood partly responsible for what happened to my family."

His eyes narrowed on her and she realized her faux pas. Her and Carrie's beliefs on what broke their family up couldn't have been more different.

"But ultimately you're right," she hurried out. "Love is for the foolish and the weak, yada-yada-yada. Let's talk about something else, remembering the heartache of time gone before is giving me goosebumps."

"Hey, I'm sorry I've upset you," he said ruefully.

"No, I'm sorry," she countered. God, she was such an idiot! "I didn't mean to snap, I just find it hard to talk about life back then. Which is totally unfair when you have told me all that you have."

Dismally, she stabbed a piece of waffle and smeared it in syrup, priming it for her mouth as she looked to force out the misery with the yumminess.

"Come here."

His command surprised her, and she popped the food into her mouth, her eyes doing the questioning for her.

"I want you to sit here," he said, gesturing to his lap as he positioned himself sideways, one arm reaching out to welcome her in.

Warmth spread through her as she pushed her plate across and sidled willingly into his lap, loving how his nearness encased her in a comfort blanket where life was altogether perfect, its effect like magic.

"Good girl," he said, pressing a kiss into her shoulder and slipping his arm about her.

She relaxed against him, and they both tucked back into food, the tension of a moment ago all but forgotten.

"You know what, though?" he said, after a while.

She shook her head on yet another mouthful.

"Having said everything I just have, I still can't help the feeling that since I got home something has changed between us."

Isla did her best to focus on the food in her mouth, her jaw working overtime to chew away the thoughts he was instilling.

"I can't stop thinking of you," he continued, his breath tickling at the skin on her shoulder. "My cock can't stop wanting you, you've ruined my kitchen with fizz and all I could do was laugh, you've got me sleeping in late and now, you have me sharing my waffles."

She looked at him on the last, unsure as to why he used the word share when he had made them for her. He spied her confusion and drew her attention to his plate, where her fork was merrily diving into *his* waffle stack. Her own plate cleared out.

She gave him an impish grin. "I told you they were good."

"That you did," he said, his gaze turning dark and hungry. Why did she get the feeling it wasn't his appetite for waffles he was thinking about anymore? "I tell you what, I'll share *my* waffles with you…if you drop the sheet."

She swallowed hard. Her eyes flaring at his words. Could she do it? Did she have the confidence to bare her body to him in the unforgiving morning light? She knew she bore marks from their love making, that her whole body smelled of their sex…

But did she care when she knew it meant having his body—that amazingly strong, hot-blooded, virtually naked body—pressed up against her own once more?

He held her gaze unflinchingly, pushing for her compliance. The heat smoldering in his smoky blue depths telling her exactly where his head was at and fuelling a confidence in her that only days before she wouldn't have thought possible.

Pushing off him, she stood and turned, her hands pausing over the secured fold of the sheet as she faced him. She saw the pulse working in his tightened jaw, his eyes burning into her fabric shield, his cock bucking in anticipation beneath his trunks…he wanted her, alright…her! Boring old Isla! The realization had her smiling from ear to ear as pointedly, she eyed his waffle stack.

He chuckled. "Ah-ah, you first."

CHAPTER NINE

IT WAS ELEVEN BY THE time he got into work. Lara was straight on him. Coffee in hand and a list of rearranged meetings from that morning. She looked pissed. And not in the alcohol sense.

"James Candy has been calling since eight," she was saying, her eyes scanning her tablet as she followed him into his office. "He's in a panic about something."

James oversaw his financial operations and was no doubt worrying about the delay in filming. "Tell him to chill, I'll get back to him this afternoon."

She nodded, stabbing at the screen. At least it wasn't just him being treated to her surprising temper this morning.

"You have your call with Hugh in five to finish going over the script I gave you yesterday," she continued, not looking up. "Since you've not had time to get to it this morning, do you want me to rearrange?"

"That makes sense." He sipped at his coffee, his brain trying to focus through the red mist surrounding Lara and the haze left by Carrie's absence. He wondered whether she too was finding it hard to concentrate without him.

"That will free you up to prep for your conference call with the Santorini team at twelve."

"Yes, that's good," he nodded absentmindedly.

"You did catch up with Chase to go through the alternative locations, didn't you?"

Chase…locations…shit! He was supposed to talk to him yesterday, to put the idea out there before the call today. What the hell was wrong with him? "No, I didn't, it completely slipped my mind."

Lara shot him an unimpressed look. "I'll go and get him on the line, shall I?"

He flinched inwardly. Christ! She really was on one today!

"Yes, please," he said, working to keep his tone level. Normally, he'd rebuke her for her attitude but considering she'd just endured a morning from Hell, courtesy of him, it didn't feel fair.

Nodding, she turned on her heel and left, taking some of the tension with her.

Bradley set his coffee down on the desk. The work-inducing drink wasn't doing its usual trick right now, when what he really needed was a total segregation from a certain part of his anatomy. Judging by Lara's mood, she'd probably help with that too. He shuddered and pushed his brain into work mode, turning on his laptop and dropping into his seat.

Lara strode back into the room, cell phone at her ear. "Okay, when he gets off set, tell him to call. It needs to be in the next thirty minutes."

She cut the call and gave him a look that screamed "idiot".

"Sorry," he said, offering what he hoped to be a disarming smile and holding up his hands in defense. "I really dropped the ball on that one."

She seemed to soften marginally, her posture relaxing. "It's okay, I guess everyone is entitled to an off day."

"Let's hope that's all it is," he said, more to himself than her.

"It's just not like you."

"No, it's not." He shifted uncomfortably in his seat, her words hitting a nerve, and he sought to change the subject. "You've been great, though, I don't know what I would do without you."

She visibly melted at the compliment, the hint of a smile playing about her lips. Perhaps he never gave her enough gratitude. What an ass!

"It's my job," she shrugged.

"Job or not, it's no excuse for me not showing you enough appreciation." He would change that, starting with now. "I know you're meeting Amy today for lunch so take a few hours off instead and go shopping with her as well. I'll drop you with her as soon as the call is done."

Her smile turned into a grin, lighting up the whole of her face. "That would be lovely, thank you."

What a relief, he felt like he could breathe again without risk of an explosion.

"No problem, her and Carrie have already started their assault on LA's finest clothing establishments so adding you into the mix may help keep them contained," he teased.

To his surprise, her smile evaporated. "I can try."

Now what was wrong? Was she jealous that the two were already spending time together shopping?

Or was she worried that the shops they were browsing were out of her pay grade? Of course they would be! He really needed to think before he spoke. "And consider the dress on me, won't you?"

"Really?" she breathed, her eyes widening, both phone and tablet looking suddenly precarious in her falling hands.

"Sure, I'll tell Amy to sort it out."

"Wow, that's so generous, thank you, Br—Mr. King!" Dizzily, she shook her head over the bumbling address, her phone and tablet safe once more as she hugged them tight to her chest.

He was about to tell her she was welcome when her cell phone started to ring.

"Chase?" he asked her as she looked at the display.

"No," she said, turning it to face him. "James."

"Here, I'll take it."

He took the phone from her outstretched palm and answered the call. "James, how goes it?"

"Bloody hell, Brad! You're the hardest man to reach."

"I'm busy, what can I say," he returned, settling back into his seat.

"Well, you're about to be even busier, Tony is threatening to pull the plug on his investment."

"What!" Now he was definitely focused, his body turning rigid, poised for action.

"I know, seems he got wind that the movie was in trouble and now he wants out."

"Who's he got that rubbish from?"

"No idea, but right now that's not the problem."

"Hold on a sec"—covering the mouth piece, he looked to Lara who was still hovering—"can you find out the whereabouts of Tony Walters? I need to pay him a visit ASAP."

She nodded, her face bright with her eagerness to help, and swept from the room.

Turning his attention back to the phone, he said, "Okay, I'll deal with it."

"You better, Brad, else you'll be bankrolling the entire thing, these things have a habit of suffering the domino effect, once one goes, the rest…"

"Yeah, yeah, I know, I'll sort it out."

"Give me a call when you do, either way give me a ring tomorrow, my heart is getting too old to deal with this shit."

"Sure thing, James, take it easy."

He ended the call, his mind well and truly where it should be—on work.

It was true he could bankroll the entire thing if he had to, but the project was a risk and it made no financial sense for him to shoulder the lot. He hadn't got where he was by taking extreme chances like that.

He just needed to pay Tony a visit and all would be well again. The project may be a risk but it didn't mean it wasn't a worthwhile one when the payback had the potential to be huge. Tony just needed reminding of that.

At least James' call had given him the focus he'd been lacking all morning.

Had Carrie been the same? Was she right now wondering what he was doing? What they'd be doing when they were next together?

And there she was, in his mind, all over again…

"How much?"

She gaped at the judgmental pharmacist, a graceful blonde who probably wasn't much older than herself and yet her holier-than-thou attitude had managed to make Isla feel more like a naughty schoolgirl than a peer. She'd thought it bad enough that she'd had to divulge pertinent facts like "when" did it happen. She hadn't even considered how expensive the itty-bitty thing would be.

Her face still burned with the shame of the conversation, her ears humming. She didn't even hear the woman repeat the cost, but blindly handed over her credit card, punching in the numbers and praying it would work. It wasn't like she was flush with cash currently. Turns out it wasn't just a foolish mistake (or mistakes, plural!), but a costly one too.

"Thank you," she said, breathing a sigh of relief as the woman passed back her card along with the box.

"Make sure you take it as soon as possible," she instructed by way of a dismissal. The woman needn't have bothered, it was the first thing Isla was planning on doing.

Exiting the pharmacy, she found herself a quiet spot on the

sidewalk and surreptitiously extracted the tablet, tossing it back with some water she had the foresight to bring.

Now she could rejoin Amy.

The poor girl had taken some convincing not to join her at the pharmacy after Isla had asked for directions. She tried to say that there was no need for her to miss out on valuable shopping time, but Amy had obviously dismissed that.

Backed into a corner, all she could tell her was that it was delicate, AKA private, and needed dealing with ASAP.

The whole "I need to go this minute" versus "don't worry about me, because I'm fine", wasn't making any sense to Amy. And quite rightly so.

Why couldn't she just have come up with a good excuse? She was such a rubbish liar. And yet, she was currently living a lie. The irony really wasn't lost on her.

"Hey, there you are!"

She turned toward the voice, Amy was skipping up to her, her eyes positively alive. "Wait until you see what I've found!"

Isla smiled, her relief at having sorted out her "predicament" having left her with a sudden rush of elation. Perhaps today could be fun. If she could keep her mind off a certain male, that is. Every time Bradley entered her head, her tummy flipped, her heart soared and her brain conjured him up with every glorious physical attribute. He was starting to scare her, to threaten her entire belief system. Even as she thought it, her pulse quickened and sweat prickled uneasily at her neck, the contradictory sensations leaving her all over the place.

"Hello, Earth to Carrie!" Amy said waving a hand in front of her face. "You going to come back to me any time soon?"

"Sorry, squirt," she blurted, guilt at her preoccupation bringing her swiftly back to the now. "I was side-tracked."

"Eurgh! Don't you start with that name too!" Amy wailed, sticking her arm through Isla's and practically dragging her along. "I bet *he's* the reason you just bailed on me too."

Oh my God! She'd sussed out her pharmacy trip. Isla could feel herself pale as she stumbled over her own feet, words escaping her.

"Easy, sis!" Amy said laughing as she steadied her off. "Let's get trying on some dresses and hopefully your brain will see fit to stay with me from here on in."

"Ah, yes, that sounds like a plan," Isla chuckled her relief as Amy's words settled on her and she realized her reference had been to her lack of concentration, not her hunt for the blasted pill. She purposefully ignored the affectionate "sis" reference. "So, I take it you've found a dress for me to see?"

"Don't be silly! I can't find a dress that quick! No, I found a sale! A really good sale!"

Sale was not a word Isla would have associated with a shopping trip conducted by someone with pockets as deep as their family but once they were in the store and she saw the price tags…

It was lucky Amy had been so engrossed in what she was trying to show her, else she would have seen the open look of horror on Isla's face. She could buy a car for that!

"Isn't it stunning?" Amy was saying.

"Yeah." What Isla really wanted to say was: what is it and where is the rest? It looked like a top but then it could also be a microscopic bin bag. There wasn't enough fabric to justify that many digits, surely!

Amy laughed. "You are so easy to read."

Isla stared at her blankly, her mind asking "in what way?" but not daring to go there, she simply shrugged instead.

"Point taken." Amy rolled her eyes as she popped it back on the display above a vintage bicycle, her attention turning to the rest of the store as her merry legs continued on their way. "Mom probably would have killed me for wearing it anyway."

Isla watched her go, her eyes scanning the dollhouse-style boutique in wonder. It really was an entirely new shopping experience for her. She didn't dare touch anything for fear of breaking something or messing up an arrangement. She really couldn't have been any further out of her comfort zone.

"I'm sensing you're not feeling this place?" Amy said, pausing in her quest through a retro convenience display to throw Isla a questioning gaze.

"Well…" How could she answer that one when the truth would give her away so completely?

"Hey, it's cool!" Amy rushed out, waving a hand in the air. "I have booked us an appointment with Mystique, anyway. We're due there in half an hour."

Isla looked at her none the wiser, and knew immediately that was a mistake.

Amy's eyes narrowed on her. "You do know Mystique, don't you?"

"Oh, yeah, sure, I thought you said something else," Isla said, trying to brush it off.

The girl shook her head at her. "You can't confuse Mystique with anything else!"—she twirled on the spot—"she's pure perfection."

Amy was lost to her now, her eyes all dreamy as she floated around the store, her hands fluttering about as she visualized their upcoming purchases. "Her team will have us fitted out in the most amazing ensemble before the day is out."

"Sounds great," Isla responded, playing catch up with the girl's excitement.

"The best bit is, Brad has given me the go-ahead to use his account! This is all on him!"

Isla swallowed. Her heart missing a beat at his name. "I don't need anything bought, I have plenty at home." Well, at Carrie's home, more accurately.

Amy gave her a grin. "If my brother says I am to treat you, then I am to treat you."

"Why? Not scared of him, are you?" Isla teased, her own face breaking into a wide grin; the girl's excitement was contagious.

Amy giggled, yanking open the door to the store and gesturing for Isla to precede her out. "Scared? You mad! That guy is as saintly as they come."

"Saintly?" Now it was Isla's turn to laugh as they left the store behind.

"You may laugh, missy," she chided with a grin, "but I tell you now, I have never seen him look at any girl like he did you when he said goodbye this morning. Yes, he may have been a bit of a bad boy in the past where women are concerned, but that guy is no more. You have totally bewitched him"—she wagged an accusing finger at her—"and if he says I am to treat you, then I better do so."

Isla swallowed again, his sister's words rocking her core. Everything she had seen of him, first-hand, laid truth to what she was telling her. But she couldn't let herself believe it. He had to be a bad boy. She *needed* him to be a bad boy.

And not bad in the sense her brain was now thinking as it pictured them entwined in the sheets, on the kitchen counter, across the sofa…

She meant it in the total alpha male, pig-headed sense, with a disgustingly fat ego and an endless string of lays to his name. That way she wouldn't fall into the trap of seeing him as anything more than a temporary figure in her life, she wouldn't run the risk of missing him when it was all over and she certainly wouldn't feel anything deeper for him.

Her heart would be safe.

"Carrie! Will you get back with me! I'm going to lose you on the sidewalk at this rate."

"I'm with you, I'm with you!" Isla hurried out, picking up her pace to bring her alongside the giddy pixie once more.

Yes, he was bad. Very, very bad…

The illicit images flooded her anew and she could feel her body coming alive. Labeling him as bad wasn't working for her. She needed to come up with something less evocative, more dick-ish, like knob or prick…and now all she could visualize was his amazing cock as he'd pulled it out in the garage!

Christ, she couldn't even mentally abuse him without it turning sexual.

"What do you think, Carrie?" Amy was asking her, about what Isla had no idea but…what did she think?

She thought keeping her mind off a certain male was going to be nigh on impossible.

That in itself should be bad thing too…it really should…

But it did make her body do amazing things: the thrumming that kick-started between her legs, the fluttering in her belly, the heat that swept her head to toe…she bit her lip to stop from humming aloud.

I'm doomed!

CHAPTER TEN

PULLING INTO THE BASEMENT PARKING lot of the downtown high rise playing host to his sister and Carrie, Brad likened his mood to suffering severe withdrawal symptoms.

He hadn't planned on getting there so late, but his calls had dragged and more had come hot on their tail.

Not only did he feel bad for Lara, whose late lunch had turned into an early finish, he had wound himself up with his inability to control his own wandering mind. He'd almost said to hell with Tony when the guy insisted they meet face to face that evening to discuss his concerns, Brad's mind and body wanting only one thing—to spend it wrapped up in some carnal escapade with the woman at the heart of his agitation. But he knew he couldn't, not in all good conscience; work dictated he saw him.

Lara eyed him curiously. "You'll bring Tony around, you know."

She obviously assumed the guy was the cause of his mood. He couldn't begin to imagine what Lara would think if she realized the true cause was the fact that he had to forego an evening with Carrie to keep Walters sweet.

"Of course I will," he acknowledged ruefully, pulling into a parking space. "The dinner was a great suggestion of yours, he was straight on it."

Color swept her cheeks. "Well, we had a good catch up while you were on with Chase. When he said he was jetting off tomorrow, it seemed like the best solution."

Best for Walters, best for the company, best for the movie, but…

"It certainly does, I'll wine and dine him and we'll be back on track," he said, then adding, more for his own benefit than Lara's, "I'll make up the time with Carrie at the party tomorrow."

"Yes, Carrie, of course," she said, turning to look out of the window. "I hadn't thought about your lack of time with her before you fly back off."

Lara may not have, but he had, and the realization was a hard one to take on board. Nerves plagued him as it begged the question "why?". Since when had he cared this much? What had changed?

"Right, let's go and see them." He undid his seatbelt and hurried out of the car, striding around to open the door for Lara.

She stepped out, her hand coming to rest on his forearm as she straightened. "Are you sure you want to buy me a dress?" she asked, sending him a look beneath her lashes, her timid attitude reminding him very much of Carrie, well, the new and distracting Carrie at any rate.

"Of course," he said, disengaging her from him as he locked the car and headed for the lift, throwing over his shoulder, "and not just a dress, I'm talking the full outfit."

Lara hurried to catch up with him. "It's incredibly kind of you, thank you."

"Don't mention it, I know I can be an ass at times, and besides, the gift is no less than you deserve." He jabbed at the lift button and stared up at the vintage dial above the doors telling him the current floor.

These things were too blasted slow.

He could feel Lara watching him and he dropped her an apologetic grimace. "Sorry to be such a grump."

"You're not a grump," she was quick to say.

"Whatever." The lift doors finally opened and he gestured for her to step inside, "Now it's you being kind."

She smiled her response, stepping in and he followed, pressing the button for the penthouse that housed Mystique's exclusive showroom. The lift's doors closed and it started its ascent, taking his pulse rate with it as his foot took up a tapping tempo.

"You're very anxious to see her."

Lara's surprise came through in her remark, and he gave her a helpless shrug. "I know, it's a weird one on me too."

He turned his attention back to the current floor display and resumed his tapping. When it finally came to a stop and the doors had opened enough to permit him through, he was out, his eagerness leaving Lara behind once more.

"Mr. King, what a pleasure to see you again," greeted the typically attractive, red-haired shop assistant primed at the entrance.

She was vaguely familiar. He scanned his memory banks, his recall skills as an actor serving him well. "Anna, it's lovely to see you too, I believe Amy is here with a friend?"

She gave him a knowing look at the friend reference and he didn't mind in the slightest, everyone knew he and Carrie were dating in these parts, even if the press hadn't gone haywire with it yet.

"Of course, this way." She included an approaching Lara in the address and gestured for them both to follow her.

They headed down the exposed brick corridor, the walls lined with artisan fabrics, mirrors, and black and white fashion photographs—an eclectic mixture clearly chosen to inspire the arriving clientele.

He saw her before she saw him, his body coming alive with an energy that he was sure everyone else in the room would be able to detect. She stood before an ornate mirror that dominated the end of one wall. The dress she was trying on, a silver sheen of fabric, fastened around her neck, leaving the majority of her back teasingly exposed and clinging to the curve of her bottom with seductive precision. It ended mid-thigh, leaving her long, lithe legs bare, their lengths made all the more alluring and arousing by the sparkling stilettos that she wore.

He cleared his throat. "That entire ensemble is coming home with us."

The words "home" and "us" came out in the same sentence before he had really thought it through. And now they were out there, he realized how good they sounded, how right and satisfying.

"Bradley!" she blurted, her eyes shooting to his in the reflection of the mirror just before she spun to face him, her balance teetering in the heels.

He was across the room in seconds, his arms soaring around her to steady her tumbling form. "Whoa! Should I take it as a compliment that you find my presence so overwhelming it's sent you to your knees?"

Her fingers ground into his arm as she clung to him for support, slowly righting herself.

"Sorry," she said, looking up at him, her cheeks flushed and eyes bright. He could see the burn of shame from her fall but more than that, he could read the excitement in her gaze and knew it mirrored his own at having her close.

"You okay?" he asked, his eyes intense on hers, their faces so close their breath entwined.

She nodded. "Just getting used to these." She gestured to the heels briefly, raising one foot off the ground, and wobbled.

He tightened his hold. "Funny, they don't seem to be that different from most others I've seen you in." Grinning, he added, "But then I'm just a man, what do I know?"

Her face seemed to burn deeper and she stepped back, forcing him to break their contact as she looked to the others in the room, her eyes homing in on Lara.

Neither girl said a word but he had the strange feeling an

unspoken exchange was taking place. And not a very amicable one at that. They had met before, it wasn't like he needed to introduce them. He would have expected at least one of them to verbally acknowledge the other. Instead, they seemed to size one another up. The very idea was ridiculous.

Amy came to the rescue, leaping up from a chaise longue she'd been occupying unnoticed by him.

"Hey, Brad, you finally made it!" She bobbed up to him and hopped on tiptoes to plant a kiss on his cheek. "And you, Lara!" she said, moving to hug the other girl. "I can't believe he kept you from me until now, I have so many things I am just desperate to show you! Haven't I, Carrie?"

"Yes, lots," Carrie agreed, her voice sounding strained and uncomfortable. "If you don't mind, I'm just going to slip out of these."

He nodded and watched her teeter off, his head worrying over the bizarre behavior.

"She does look amazing, doesn't she?"

The question came from the shop assistant who had joined him.

"Indeed," he said, looking to her now that Carrie had disappeared to change. "Can I have that entire outfit sent over to her house? Tomorrow morning at the latest?"

She beamed up at him. "Of course, Mr. King."

"And whatever these two decide upon," he said, turning to look at Lara and Amy. "I've already told Amy to put it on my account."

The girl nodded, her face positively glowing. "Right then, ladies, shall we?" she prompted, gesturing for the two of them to follow her.

Amy glanced his way. "What's your plan?"

"I'm going to take Carrie out for a bit, do you want me to swing by in a couple of hours to take you both home?"

"Nah, Lara and I can take care of ourselves, you two lovebirds go and enjoy yourselves," she gave him a wink.

"Thanks for the offer though," Lara said, giving him a smile that didn't quite meet her eyes. Considering where she was and what she was about to purchase, the girl was very subdued.

"You feeling okay?" he asked her.

Amy put her head between the two of them, her attention on Lara as she blocked his view of her. "She's fine, Brad! How could she not be?" she stressed. "We're about to spend a chunk of your hard-earned cash, what could be more thrilling?"

He heard Lara give a small chuckle. "Absolutely."

"Catch ya later, big bro," Amy fired at him as she pulled Lara away to follow the awaiting shop assistant.

"Have fun!" he said.

Lara gave him a look over her shoulder and a small wave. "Thanks again."

"No problem."

Watching the two girls walk away, he was relieved to hear their excited chatter start up, the awkwardness of a moment before gratefully forgotten. It was important to him that Lara be happy, almost as much as it was for him to see Amy happy.

"Your adoration is very endearing." The sound of Carrie's voice washed over him and he turned to see her walking toward him, her body back in the tight jeans and white shirt he had left her in that morning.

"Adoration..." he smiled over the word. "They both have a very special place in my heart, it's true."

"Both?" she said, an edge to her voice now as she paused next to him, her eyes trained on the three women perusing the clothes rail across the room.

He eyed her. "Not jealous, are we?"

"Of Amy? No, she is your sister." She shifted uneasily, clearly not happy with the words she was uttering. "But Lara? Is it normal to have such affection for an employee?"

"There's history there," he said simply, wondering how much he should tell her.

Now she looked at him, her expression unreadable. "I don't think she likes me very much."

"That's not true," he said automatically but the words nagged at him. He knew there was something amiss between them and he didn't really want to think on it too much.

"Shall we go?' she said suddenly. "I don't think I need a new outfit."

"We can go, but you're not leaving without something."

"I really don't need anything and I'm shopped out," she complained. "Please, let's just go, I'm ready for home."

He studied her for a moment, wondering whether he should tell her he'd already arranged for the outfit to be sent. She didn't really seem in the receptive mood and knew it was down to Lara. He needed to explain the situation but not here, not with an audience.

"Sure." He offered her his arm and she hooked her own through, her attention forcibly on the lift to which they now headed. "But I'm not taking you home, I'm taking you for a drink, ever since I let you out of my sight this morning my day went south and now I have an evening that needs to be spent entertaining an investor."

They entered the awaiting lift that a shop attendant had already called for. He nodded his gratitude and waited for the doors to close before he turned her into him, lifting her chin so that she faced him. "Please tell me you will allow me to take you out so that I can at least have a little fun before then?"

He saw the indecision in her eyes and gently pressed a kiss to her forehead, his hand slipping to the back of her neck. He felt the breath escape her lips on a sigh and smiled, pressing another kiss to her brow, the bridge of her nose, then the tip…

"Please," he whispered as his mouth found her own, the fullness of her bottom lip settling above his.

She whimpered as her mouth parted. He didn't need any further encouragement, his mouth claimed hers in a hungry kiss that wiped out the last few hours, taking him back to that morning at breakfast, her body molding into him as she let him take all that he wanted and more.

Neither of them noticed the lift doors opening until a bemused couple coughed at the lift entrance, waiting to get in.

He tightened his hold on Carrie's waist, scared that she was going to hit the deck as her body leaned into him so entirely.

"Excuse us," he said to the couple as he escorted Carrie out, past the pair and into the basement parking lot.

Bowing his head to her ear, he whispered, "Perhaps taking us back to mine would be a better idea, might save others having to endure us?"

"No!"

Her quick-fired response surprised him and he stopped to look at her.

"Sorry," she said with a small smile, her hand coming up to brush her hair away from her face. "I'm just starved, I've not eaten since breakfast and could do with something now, let's go somewhere local."

"Fair enough," he said, trying to mask his disappointment. "I know just the place and then we can talk, I think I should explain the Lara thing."

"You really don't have to," she said, but her eyes told him otherwise.

CHAPTER ELEVEN

SHE DIDN'T REALLY WANT TO eat, she didn't even want to drink, what she wanted to do was understand what twisted relationship he had with his PA. She must be half his age!

The way the girl had looked at her had painted a thousand words, all of them laced with a jealous loathing.

Combined with the open affection he clearly held for Lara, and topped off with his mention of "history", her brain had gone racing off to its own merry conclusion.

The last place she wanted to be was in his home and, ultimately, in his bed.

She had decided that afternoon that alone time with him was no longer a good idea. That she needed to avoid it as much as possible. His increasing effect on her, her inability to stop thinking about him, and her impending exit from his world, meant that all sense dictated she protect herself by limiting her exposure to him. And when avoidance of him wasn't possible, then at the very least she needed to stick to being out in public, forcing him to maintain a certain level of behavior and giving her a chance at keeping her body in check.

Christ, even when she was full of distaste for his questionable relationship with Lara, she still couldn't stop her body responding to him. The lift escapade had just proved that, unequivocally.

No, private time was to be a definite no!

She looked around the discreet booth they currently occupied in the exclusive wine bar and decided that even this was too private. His thigh pressed electrifyingly against hers as he sat beside her, holding the menu out so that she could choose her fancy.

She couldn't even imagine tasting any of it. She just wanted him to confess all so that she could at least inform Carrie of his misdemeanors with Miss Attitude. When all was said and done, it made no odds to her if he had been conducting some sordid affair under her sister's nose. Honest.

"If you slide any more to the right you are going to end on the floor," he said, the nearness of his voice resonating through her and making her insides quiver in treacherous delight.

Disregarding his warning, she shuffled away once more and sure enough, found herself hovering over the edge.

"For goodness sake, Carrie," he grumbled, forcefully slipping his arm down her back so that he could press his hand to her thigh and draw her up against him, the protective power in his hold turning the quiver into a full-blown fire. "Perhaps you'll relax enough to choose food if I tell you about Lara."

"Like I said," her voice sounded almost childlike in its pitch, "you don't need to."

At that moment, a waiter appeared with a bottle and two glasses. "Your usual, sir."

Usual? How of often did he come here? Did he come with *her*?

"Thank you, Tom."

First name terms too, clearly it was often!

She knew she was being ridiculous. Knew she had no right to be jealous. Knew he wasn't even hers to be jealous of. She could pretend it was anger for Carrie that had her in such a tizz, but she'd be lying to herself. As she was swiftly learning, it wasn't just her body that was betraying her, it was her heart and mind too.

Tom poured them both a glass and discreetly left. She eyed the appealing red liquid and realized it was probably just what she needed.

Bradley read her mind, taking up her glass and handing it to her. "It's good, I promise."

She sipped at the drink. It was good. It warmed her from the inside, calming her rampaging thoughts enough to realize that she owed him the chance to explain. She also realized that, real reason aside, she needed him to explain, to hopefully make her understand it wasn't as bad as she feared.

"Okay, it's obvious you're dying to tell me," she said, trying to sound nonplussed and failing miserably. "I'm all ears."

He chuckled softly. "I think I'll take it as a positive sign that you're this unsettled by my relationship history," he said, his arm around her relaxing as he must have felt the imminent danger of her bolting had passed. "It's certainly never bothered you before, perhaps it's a sign of how your feelings are evolving too?"

Too? What did he mean "too"? Were his feelings changing? Is that what he had meant that morning when he had said things were different between them since he had gotten back? And in what way? Her head was spinning with all the possibilities, their magnitude leaving her dizzy as she failed to answer him, taking instead a steadying sip of her drink.

"I'm going to take your silence as a yes," he said, giving her a meaningful look that she couldn't quite meet. "Hey, come on, we'll get this Lara conversation dealt with and then all will be right again, okay?"

She managed to give him a nod and, happy to have her consent, he gave her a squeeze, his free hand taking up his wine glass. "Things with Lara are different because she didn't come to me as a typical employee."

"No?' Isla said, finally able to look at him now that his attention was on his glass, his hand rotating the stem to swirl the wine within.

"Not at all, I came across Lara at rehab with Amy. My sister had been in a really bad way for a while. Even after the withdrawal symptoms had subsided, she was low. The counselors and therapists were all doing their best, but she had no spark anymore. It's when I truly understood the term 'a shadow of one's former self' and it was a really sad time…"

His voice trailed off and he took a sip of his wine, his face pained and contemplative. She shivered internally. She couldn't imagine the Amy she knew now without her delightful bubble and bounce. It must have killed him to see.

"Look, we don't need to talk about this," she said compulsively, not wanting him to relive it.

He looked down at her, his eyes soft, the hint of a smile touching his lips. "Oh, I think I do, it's important to me that you understand."

She was captivated by his look, vulnerable yet masterful all at the same time, and she felt her heart swell.

I really am doomed…

"Okay," she said, lowering her gaze and settling into the crook of his arm, her ears listening while her mind tried to keep her grounded.

"I would visit her every few days," he continued, "they didn't like you to be there too much, they believed their guests needed to learn to be strong without their loved ones being there twenty-four-seven. But slowly she seemed to get better. At first I thought it was the treatment plan…don't get me wrong, that obviously played a huge part…but then she started speaking of this friend she'd made, how they'd hit it off and together they were helping one another."

"Lara?" she asked as it all clicked into place.

He nodded. "Yes. At first, I was wary, the idea of addicts being friends didn't sit well with me. But then I saw them together, I saw how vulnerable Lara was and how Amy helped her and in so doing regained her own strength." He shrugged. "I was sold, so to speak."

"When they came out of rehab, Amy asked if I would take Lara on, convinced the role would help keep her focused on recovery. I think we both could see a helplessness in her, she didn't have a family to speak of and her friends were what got her into trouble in the first place, so I guess you could say we welcomed her into our unit. And to be fair, she has even been great for me too. She's brilliant at her job, devoted to it really, and is great for Amy."

"It certainly explains a lot," Isla said, absorbing his words, her heart obliterating her cruel jealous ramblings as it exploded with sympathy, warmth and understanding. Instinctively, she raised her head and pressed a kiss into his cheek. "Turns out you have a heart of gold, Mr. King."

"Hey, easy, that wasn't what you were thinking five minutes ago."

Her cheeks burned. "To hell with what I thought then, they were the thoughtless ramblings of a jealous girlfriend and I take it all back."

"I wouldn't take it *all* back. Recent events are starting to make me realize I may have an issue where Lara is concerned."

"What issue?" she asked, even though she knew the answer really.

"I know I said that you were wrong to think she doesn't like you very much, but truth is, she's been out of sorts of late and only where you're concerned," he said, raising his glass to his lips, his brow furrowed in concern.

"I don't like to say it, but I think she's head over heels for you."

He choked on his drink mid-swig. "That's a bit much. I'm old enough to be her father."

"And?"

"Well, I've treated her like a little sister for so long now, she's probably just jealous of the time both Amy and I have spent with you, she probably feels pushed out," he said, his voice full of conviction. "And she's certainly not used to a girlfriend taking up so much of my time, both when I'm with you and when I'm not."

"When you're not? What's that supposed to mean?"

"It means that currently even my work is in jeopardy where you're concerned. My brain is following you around whether you're physically present or conjured up in my imagination."

She smiled at that. The realization that he was just as affected as she triggering a giddiness that she couldn't talk down. She could almost believe his feelings were all meant for her too. The real her—Isla, not Carrie.

Almost, but not quite.

"What will you do about her?" she asked.

"No idea, but right now all I care about is enjoying this time with you before we have to part again." He pressed a kiss to her hair. "Now choose something, you must be famished."

She did as he instructed and selected a feast that would satisfy her stressed-out tummy, forcing herself to relax and live in the moment, just for a little while longer.

He entertained her with tales that seemed to come so easily to him and she told her own from a childhood that both her and Carrie had shared.

He watched her eat, his expression one of approval and growing arousal. He obviously liked that she had an appetite and that she liked to share, frequently forking a piece to feed to him. Although that was less about sharing and more about the delicious sensation between her legs each time she watched him take the food in, the move deliberately slow, his evocative eyes trained on her and making it clear it was her he'd rather be devouring.

"You need to stop doing that," she said, her words catching as she slid a spoon of chocolate soufflé from his closed mouth. His tongue slipping out to discreetly clear the remnants on his lips but not discreetly enough that it didn't inspire a zillion thoughts of what she wanted that tongue to be doing to her.

She spooned a piece into her own mouth. The rich chocolate was a heady assault on her taste buds as it mixed with the sexual need mounting inside her.

"What?" he asked in mock innocence, his hand dropping to her knee beneath the table.

"You know exactly what," she breathed, the heat of his touch sending sparks through her.

"How about I do this instead?" he asked, his hand travelling up the inside of her thigh and causing her to tense on a rush of excitement.

"*Behave!*" she stressed, her hand coming down to stop the progression of his, her eyes scanning the restaurant for onlookers.

"No one can see," he assured her, his smile wickedly appealing as his fingers began to massage into her skin.

This couldn't be happening.

Not here!

"Bradley," she whispered his name, the sound drawn out as she struggled to breathe, the telltale heat between her legs screaming her body's readiness for him.

"I love how you say my name," he said, his gaze dark and hungry as it dropped to her mouth, his hand easing up her thigh once again and taking her meekly resisting hand with it.

She was lost to his look, to his touch, even the feel of her hand as it helplessly tracked his own. He got to the apex of her thigh and she whimpered, the spoon she still held falling from her grasp to clash with the plate.

Her eyes shot down to the noise and then around to the room. She felt like the world knew what he was doing to her—what she was letting him do! But in reality, everyone was deeply involved in their own conversations. The only person that even breathed in their direction was the waiter, Tom.

Bradley kept up his caress, even as she tensed once more beneath him, and to her virtuous-horror, he gestured the waiter over. She sent him a look that told him "stop, but don't stop" all at the same time. It was a conflicting message he well understood as he gave her that smile once more.

He turned to face the approaching waiter, his hand unceasing in its attentions beneath the table. "Tom, we're in a hurry, can you charge it to my account, please?"

To her amazement, the chap made no show that he was aware of anything untoward occurring and yet she felt like her whole body screamed her arousal.

"Of course, sir, was everything to your liking?"

"Very much so," Bradley assured him, flicking her a look that spoke of the double meaning to his words. "What say you, Carrie?"

"Yes, it was lovely," she said, offering the waiter a small smile and praying her skin wasn't as flushed at it felt.

"Excellent, we hope to see you again very soon." He gave a brief nod and disappeared off as discreetly as he had arrived.

"Shall we?" Bradley said, his fingers sliding up over her fastened jean zipper and sending her virtually leaping from the table as she nodded at him.

She thought he might laugh at her skittish move, but one look at his face and she could see he was struggling to keep a lid on his own need.

Just once more, I'll have him just once more, and then I'll stop.

Their burning desire had them at the parking lot and in the car in record time. As she slipped into the seat and moved to take hold of the seatbelt, he stilled her hand. "Not yet, you don't."

His lips were on hers instantly, his hand thrusting through her hair. "I can't wait any longer," he said, his voice hoarse. "I need to see you come, to hear my name slip from your lips while your body is racked with your desire for me."

She moaned, the sound echoing through the car. "But there are people!" she said as she tried to keep a handle on reality.

"And we have privacy glass," he responded, his mouth now nipping at her neck as he worked to undo the buttons on her shirt.

Hell, who was she kidding, the whole of LA could be watching them right now and she couldn't and wouldn't stop him.

"Undo your jeans," he commanded as he spread open her shirt.

Her thought to refuse lasted a nanosecond at most, obliterated as soon as he slipped his hand over one aching breast, her body thrusting upward in thrilling delight.

Blindly, she found the button on her fly and popped it open, her fingers working the zip next. He unclasped the front fastening of her bra, the fabric falling to the side and exposing her nipples to the tantalizing fresh air.

"You are beautiful," he said as his mouth found one swollen nub, his teeth and tongue creating a sensational mix of pain and pleasure.

His hands shoved at the fabric of her jeans, creating just enough space to slip his hand beneath her panties and then he was upon her, his skillful fingers providing the perfect circling pressure over her throbbing clit.

She cried out, her hands gripping him through his hair, holding his attention on her breasts. Her legs tensing up as he took up the ideal tempo between her legs.

"I can't…I can't…" She wanted to tell him she couldn't take much more, but she couldn't even get those words out. Her hands flung out to her sides and she gripped at the car, desperately trying to take control of the earth-shattering sensation within.

"Say my name, baby," he said heatedly against her. "Say it!"

Christ! She wasn't going to say it, she was going to scream it!

As the rush of her climax took hold, his name left her. With each mind-blowing wave, she said it again. And as it ebbed away and her body collapsed into the seat, she brought his head to hers, her lips finding his own as she kissed him long and hard.

"Thank you, Bradley," she whispered eventually, her eyes taking in his desire-filled gaze.

"*Fuck, Carrie!*" he said, his voice wracked with desire, his hand moving to adjust his jeans. "What are you doing to me?"

Everything about him screamed need. She couldn't leave him like that. But she couldn't very well let him come inside her. She didn't think she could stomach another pharmacy trip.

"Nothing yet," she teased, the words delivered almost shyly as she thought about what she could do.

He looked at her questioningly.

"It's your turn to undo your jeans," she said, confidence growing within her.

He smiled, the excitement from him palpable as he fell back into his seat and did as she asked.

Her eyes dropped to the hardness of him, pressing through the confines of his underwear and suddenly she was hungry for him.

Lowering her head, she slipped her hand inside his parted jeans and felt him buck into her palm, his breath hissing out as she let her hand slip further still to cup his balls, her fingers gently toying with them as her other hand worked to bring his underwear down, exposing the rigid length of him to her ravenous gaze.

God, he was rock solid for her!

The sight had her excitement returning tenfold and she gripped her hand around him, moving it over him with fascinating contemplation: could she really fit all of him inside her? Was her mouth truly that big?

She hovered over him, her tongue flicking out to tease at his tip. He gasped and bucked at the move, sending her confidence sky-high. She did it again, this time letting her hand travel the length of him while her tongue flicked and teased.

He trembled beneath her, liquid pooling at his tip. Enthralled, she dipped her tongue to taste him, the saltiness an erotic delight. She didn't want to wait any longer, she wanted to fill her mouth with as much of him as possible, to feel him move within her and have him lose his control.

Positioning her mouth at his head, she parted her lips and slid over him.

"*Carrie!*" he cried, his hands shooting to her hair.

She hummed around him in response, loving how powerful she felt, how dominant, how he was completely at her mercy in that moment. She brought her head up, sucking him back as she went.

A strangled groan escaped his throat.

"You like that?" she asked, her mouth hovering just over him.

"*Fuck yes!*"

She did it again, sending him to the back of her throat, so deep she struggled for air, getting high on the arousing effect she was having on him and on herself in return. She picked up her pace, one hand still cupping his balls, her other working over him alongside her mouth with increasing ferocity.

His breathing turned ragged, his hands fisting in her hair, his roughness growing with his fast approaching climax and she was lost with him, her own desire mounting as she fed off his.

She tasted salt once more, knew it was a sign he was at the brink and then he exploded, her name tearing from his mouth as he filled her with his seed. The hot liquid shooting inside her as she drunk him down. She made sure she drained him of every last drop, her mouth slowly moving over him now as he spilled his fill and when he became sensitive to her move she raised her head to his, her mind and body warming under the blatant affection in his gaze.

"You have just made one man very happy," he said gruffly, a hand coming up to brush her hair from her face. "That's a first for us."

A first?

Isla had to work hard to keep a mask of happiness in place as inside reality came crashing down upon her. It was a first for him and Carrie, and she wasn't to know exactly what that first was. To go down on him or to swallow? Or to do it in a car? She shuddered, she couldn't help it. The thought of him with her, the knowledge that this would soon be a distant memory, the reminder that she was lying to him. She died inside.

"Hey, you don't seem very happy about it," he said, concern filling his gaze as his eyes scanned her face.

She looked away, settling back into her seat. "I'm just sad that the evening has to come to an end," she whispered.

"Me too, but there's always tomorrow."

She nodded, incapable of saying anything else as a lump formed in her throat. She distracted herself by righting her clothes and he did the same.

"Let's get you home," he said, cupping her face gently to give her one last look before starting up the engine.

She turned to gaze out the window, horrified to feel the tears start to fall. Silently, she wiped them away, doing her damnedest to keep Bradley from noticing.

They spent the journey to Carrie's house in complete silence. If Bradley found it strange, he didn't say anything, not until they stood on the doorstep saying goodbye.

He studied her, his expression serious. "Do you want to tell me what's bothering you?"

"It's nothing," she said, shaking her head, her eyes not meeting his. "I'm just being silly."

"I don't believe that."

He stroked her cheek, and she moved her head into the caress. "I just don't want you to go," she murmured, saying the thing that was at the forefront of her mind.

He smiled, his expression softening. "Well, if it helps, I'm going to miss you too."

She melted at his words, her lips finding his in a desperate need to feel close to him once more.

He kissed her back, the passion between them reigniting full force and for a split second she thought he would stay. And she would have let him.

To hell with the consequences and judgmental blonde pharmacists!

But he pulled back, a growl of frustration deep in his throat. "Is that you making doubly sure that I spend the meeting thinking of you instead of work?"

"Maybe," she said, giving him a coy smile as she pushed open the door.

"You are a tease, Miss Evans," he said on a chuckle before turning on his heel to head back to his car. "It's just one of the many reasons I find myself falling for you."

She froze midway through entering the house, her heart in her mouth. He hadn't just said that. He hadn't. He really hadn't.

He had.

CHAPTER TWELVE

H E LOOKED LIKE HE'D NOT slept. Bradley's reflection in the bathroom mirror as he toweled himself off told him as much, even a decent shave and a slap of hair product wasn't really going to help. But at least he would feel like he'd made the effort to look decent for the party that evening. Not that Marie herself would care, he could look like he was on his deathbed and she wouldn't bat an eye, so long as she got what she needed out of the evening.

He flung the towel aside and buried the thought. She wasn't the woman he was out to impress anyway. And she wasn't the reason he'd failed to get a decent night's sleep either.

No, it was all about Carrie. She'd been in his mind almost constantly. From the point he'd left her house, throughout his successful dinner with Walters, the drive home, to his dreams that night. He'd slept badly. Each time he woke he reached for her, the scent of her on his sheets tricking his sleep-filled mind and body into believing she was there.

This couldn't continue. He needed to ask her to move in if he was going to find peace again. He should have suggested it long before he'd proposed, maybe she would have given him a straight "yes" then.

He circled shaving foam over his skin and took up the razor, his thoughts turning to the proposal once more. It plagued him that she hadn't given him an answer yet. She hadn't even given him one after he'd raised it in the bath. In fact, that had only seemed to incense her…which, in itself, hadn't been all bad as the stirring of his cock had him recalling, in all its graphic detail.

Oh, yes, they were fucking great together…so, what was her problem?

It could only be down to the way he had gone about it. He certainly hadn't been traditional. *Christ, I didn't even ask her father's permission!*

He hissed as the razor nipped his jaw line, its angle offset as the severity of his mistake hit home.

What a jackass!

He leaned into the mirror to assess the damage, a small nick, nothing too awful. Not like his bloody proposal. Carrie may not be an old romantic, but she still respected her father's wishes and valued his opinion in almost everything. He should have involved him from the outset.

There was nothing he could do to change the past, but he sure as hell could put things right. He was convinced their relationship was heading somewhere neither of them had thought possible, and he owed her a proper proposal. Not one that came with the shoddy reasoning he had given previously.

A plan emerging, he finished up his shave and headed into the bedroom. Chucking on the first clothes that came to hand, he headed for the office, keen to get things underway.

Lara was in high spirits when he arrived, which surprised him, considering her recent tumultuous behavior.

"Good morning, Mr. King," she greeted as he walked in, his coffee ready and waiting in her outstretched palm. "I hear everything is back on track with Tony Walters."

He took the coffee and gave her a smile. "Thanks. Yes, it's full steam ahead."

He started to move off, but then stopped, his recent insight into her peculiar conduct making him pause to ask, "More importantly, did you get yourself an outfit?"

She blushed. "I did, thank you!"

"That's excellent news." His attempt at being thoughtful was clearly going down well. Top marks there! "So, I take it you will be heading off early to get ready?'

She blushed deeper at the suggestion. "Well, Amy has booked her and Carrie in to have their hair done beforehand."

"Sounds good," he said, his body warming at the mention of Carrie's name, his mind threatening to wander. Clearing his throat, and forcing his attention to stay put for a second more, he asked, "And what about you?"

"Well, she did ask if I could maybe join them?"

"Of course, you should," he said easily. "You leave whenever you need to."

She was positively beaming now. That ought to do it. A happy Lara, leaving early to get ready with her best friend. Now, he could hopefully get on the pressing subject of Carrie without too much upset. Heading to his desk, he set his coffee down and dropped into his seat.

Lara had followed him in and stood waiting on the other side of the desk, ready for her first instruction of the day. He had two: "Please, can you get me Carrie's father on the line, I need to speak with him as soon as possible." The man was a busy film producer, but hopefully the mention of his name would be enough to demand his swift attention. "Then can you check with Mystique to see if Carrie has received the outfit?"

His approach to focus on her before moving onto Carrie had served him well, she didn't appear affronted in the slightest. Giving him a brief nod, she piped, "Right away," and hurried off. It was a definite improvement, a good sign, for sure.

Feeling buoyed, he picked up his cell phone to check for any messages. He'd hoped to see something from Carrie, but there was nothing.

He started to type her a message and stopped. He was a grown man for goodness sake, he could wait until the evening to speak with her.

He was still debating with himself when Lara returned, talking as she tapped away on her tablet. "His PA says she will get him to call you later today if she can, he's out on location this morning and isn't contactable."

"Fair enough," he nodded. "Mystique?"

"They confirmed it's in transit. It should be with her within the hour."

"Great! Thank you, Lara."

He smiled as he thought of the surprise on her face when she received it.

Maybe he would hear from her then.

He really, really hoped so.

Yet again, Isla found herself making nice with Carrie's voicemail. She'd known it unlikely that she would reach her before bed, but she had hoped to at least wake the next morning to her sister returning her call. The message she had left, once again, made it clear that it was urgent, but there wasn't even a text message to say she'd got it and would be in touch.

She hadn't worked out exactly what she was going to say, but what she did know was that it had gone from telling her they had ended up in bed together again, to a lot more. She now had to confess she had feelings for him. And that if his words had been anything to go by, he felt the same way about *her*! And her, as in Isla. And not her, as in Carrie.

Would her sister simply laugh? It was crazy, after all. Why would he fall for her, when he hadn't even fallen for her far more glamorous and successful counterpart? The very idea was unbelievable.

So, was she deluded? Had the past few days just gone to her head and she had lost sight of reality?

She wandered into the kitchen and was immediately struck by the flower arrangement he had bought her after their first encounter. So much had happened since then. She felt like it was weeks ago and yet it was only a couple of days. How could one's life turn around so dramatically in such a short space of time?

She poured herself a fresh cup of coffee and took Carrie's phone to the breakfast bar, ready to dial her once more.

The buzz of the intercom stopped her.

Oh my God, he can't be here!

She shot off the stool and checked her appearance in the nearest mirror. She hadn't even washed yet, her face showing every bit of her lost sleep. Then she realized he wouldn't buzz, he would enter like he owned the place, just like he had done previous.

Her heart sunk and she pressed the intercom. "Who is it?"

"I have a delivery for Carrie Evans," came a male voice.

A delivery? She hadn't ordered anything on Carrie's behalf. Perhaps, her sister had ordered her something by way of an apology…unlikely…

"Sure, one sec." She released the gate for him to enter the grounds and opened the front door ready to relieve him of the delivery.

She watched as he pulled up in the van, hopped out and headed to the back. Swinging open the doors, he extracted a box, followed by a clothes bag.

She knew immediately what it was. Her guess confirmed as he got closer and she spotted the intricate Mystique logo engraved on the front of the package. Her heart stopped and she just gaped.

He smiled and gave her mute form the once-over. "So, lady, would you like me to take them in for you?"

"Can you actually take them back?" was her knee-jerk response.

He looked at her like she was mad. "No can do, I just get paid to deliver, if you have a problem with them, you need to take them back yourself or arrange another courier."

"Of course, sorry." Reluctantly, she took them from him like they were made of china.

"I just need your signature."

Right, signature. "One sec."

She hooked the clothes bag on a coat peg next to the door and put the shoe box on the floor. Returning to take up his pen and pad. Her hand scribbling "I. Evans" before she had even thought about it. Not that anyone would question it really. It was just a scribble at the end of the day. But just another reminder of how she had lied to the sender.

"Thank you," she said, passing the pad back to him, her hands trembling.

"No problem, lady."

And then he was gone, and she was left once more with her thoughts. She closed the door and leaned back against it.

Ultimately, it didn't matter that Bradley had said he was falling for her. All that would be over once he learned of her deception.

She noticed the card hanging off the clothes bag. Nervously, she lifted it off and opened it.

Please humor me. I can't wait to see you in it tonight. Brad x

She clutched the note to her chest, her stomach churning. She had to get hold of Carrie.

Striding to the phone, she dialed her sister and was relieved to hear it stop mid-ring as a rather breathless Carrie answered, "Isla! So sorry, I'm here, can you hear me?"

She could, but only just, the noise in the background gave the impression that her sister was on a building site. "I can, just about, where are you?"

"Out with Dan, it's a long story. What's going on? Are you okay? I am so relieved you've called, after our last conversation you had me so worried…"

A small part of her wanted to quiz her about Dan and exactly where they were, but it was so far from the forefront of her concerns that she pushed the thought aside.

"You can forget our last conversation, Carrie, things have moved on since then."

"In what way?" she asked warily. "Isla? Are you okay? You don't sound okay?"

"No, I'm not," she wanted to cry, she could feel it stuck in her throat and pricking at the backs of her eyes.

"Hang on, let me get somewhere more quiet." The sound became muffled as her sister must have covered the mouth piece but she could still make out her speaking, "I need to take this call somewhere quiet, it's important, Isla doesn't sound good."

She heard a male respond, more than likely Dan. "Okay, use the office."

The office? Were they at one of his clubs? Why would Carrie need to be with him at work?

Stick with the program, Isla!

Getting distracted by Dan and Carrie's antics wasn't going to help her get anything off her chest, and she needed to, before she exploded with it.

The noise gradually subsided and Carrie's voice returned to the call. "Sorry, love, I'm here now. Tell me everything."

It all came rushing out, some of it more candid than she'd wanted, but once she'd started, she hadn't been able to hold back. To at last be honest felt so good.

Finally, she came up for air and waited for Carrie's reaction, her sister hadn't made the faintest noise throughout, her silence shredding Isla's nerves.

"I can't tell you how much I hate myself right now," her sister said, her self-loathing the last thing Isla expected to get.

"What are you talking about?"

"Listen to me, Isla, you need to tell him you're sick, you can't go to that party tonight. You need to get yourself on the next flight home and let me deal with the rest."

"Let you deal with the rest...?" Isla said dumbly. "Are you not listening to what I'm saying? I'm crazy about him and I think, from what he has said, he feels something for me too. Something he didn't feel when he was with you."

Her sister gave a hard laugh. "Earth to Isla—are you hearing yourself?"

"Yes, I can hear myself," Isla forced out, her eyes clamping shut as she refused to let the meaning behind Carrie's sarcasm hit home. She drew in a deep breath and opened her eyes to take in the note he had sent, her heart warming with hope as she said, "You know what, sis, I thought maybe you would give me a nice pep talk on how he may take it badly, but if it's meant to be, it will all work out. The last thing I expected was a 'run for your life' spiel. Are you sure you're not just jealous?"

"Look, this isn't some fairy tale," Carrie said harshly. "You, of all people, know those kind of happy ever afters don't exist. Least of all in Hollywood and not with a man like Brad."

"I may have thought that before," she said honestly, "but now, I don't know, I've never felt like this about someone."

Her sister muttered something under her breath, she thought she could make out Dan's name, but before Isla could question her, she piped up again, "It doesn't matter how you feel about him anyway"—Isla audibly gasped but Carrie continued on regardless—"what matters is, that he does *not* love you, no matter what he has said."

"Perhaps the fact that *you* are unable to love anyone, makes *you* believe that to be the case, but I don't. He told me he was falling for me, has he ever said that to you?"

"They're just words."

"Words with a hell of lot of meaning, sis."

"Words, Isla! Just words!" She could feel her sister's frustration down the phone. "You need to listen to me, I *know* him!"

"And I don't?"

Carrie scoffed. "It's been a few days."

"And we've talked, a lot."

"Whatever, I've known him a hell of a lot longer than you."

Ouch!

What could she really say to that? Could she really argue that she knew him better, regardless of the timeframe? Could she really dismiss all those months, maybe even years, that him and Carrie had spent with one another? After all, she had no idea how long their relationship had been going on for, and neither did she want to find out now. It left her feeling sick.

"Look, Isla, I'm sorry," Carrie's voice came down the line again, this time softer, and to Isla's chagrin, full of pity. "In truth, you are far more lovable than me, and, if the man was capable of love, then, yes, I believe wholeheartedly that he would fall for you."

The endearment behind her sister's words had her eyes welling up. "But?" She knew there was a but.

"*It's just not him, darling,*" she said. "It wasn't me, either, it's why we worked on some level."

Worked on some level—had that really been enough to make them happy? It was just so sad, all of it.

"Isla, please speak to me."

She opened her mouth to say something, but nothing came out. Her vision blurred and she felt the first tear roll down her cheek. She looked to the dress bag and then the note in her hand once more. Could he really have said and done everything he had, and not fallen—even just a little—in love with her?

"I am so sorry," her sister said into the silence. "I can't believe any of this has happened. I feel awful for putting you in this position, I never should've—"

"I have to go, Carrie." She needed to go, she couldn't listen to her sister's negativity anymore. It was crushing her.

"Please, Isla, don't go like this, I hate the thought of you being there alone and in pain. I wish I was there."

"Well, you're not." Thank goodness. Isla didn't think she could cope with her sister's perfect presence right now.

"What about dad, have you seen him yet?"

Really? She wants to bring him up now?

"I've told you I'm not interested in seeing him."

"But I asked you to tell him about our switch, I put it in the rules."

Ah, yes, the last few rules that Isla chose not to examine too closely. She couldn't help the manic laugh that erupted. "I know you did, sis, and I purposefully ignored that bit. I figured you would let him know eventually."

"But that's not the point," Carrie stressed. "I wanted to be sure you saw him, spent some time with him."

"If you're still trying to make me feel better, you're going the wrong way about it."

"But he's our dad, Isla, he'd love to see you, and he can at least help take your mind off this disastrous turn of events…until you can get yourself home, that is."

Isla could feel her temper rising with the tears and she fought to keep it in check. She didn't want to fall out with Carrie over their father, not on top of everything else that was going wrong. "Seeing dad is not high on my list of priorities, clearing my conscience is."

"Look, telling Brad the truth isn't going to help matters," Carrie sounded almost panicked now. "You'd be better lying low and getting yourself back here as soon as possible. Let me pick up the pieces."

"I'll think about it."

"Please don't do anything rash, Isla."

"I've told you, I'll think about it." Her tone brooked no argument and she silently pleaded that Carrie would get the hint.

"Okay…I know I don't have any right to make you do what I want, you have to do what's right for you, but please, call me again when you've made your decision?"

"I will."

They said their goodbyes and Isla collapsed into the sofa, her head in her hands. What a mess things had become. It would be okay if her heart hadn't got wrapped up in it all. But now she cared. Too much.

She didn't move for an age, her mind tossing possibilities around until she felt she was going in circles. There was one thing for sure, she couldn't leave LA without him knowing the truth, about who she was and just how much she felt for him. That way she could at least create the possibility of a future for them.

No matter what Carrie had said, she just couldn't believe that what he'd told her were just words, that there was no deeper feeling underlying them.

She was desperate to get it off her chest, desperate to see what the future truly had in store, but she could hardly do it today, of all days, when Amy's happiness and, ultimately, Bradley's hinged on the party being a success. No, she would have to wait until tomorrow.

But the thought of seeing him again and not confessing all was nigh on impossible. Attending the party and acting like everything was fine…it just wasn't in her. She wasn't the actress her sister was. She knew if she saw or spoke to him, it would all come rushing out as it had done with Carrie.

No, she had to bail on the party and leave it as late as possible to tell Amy. She didn't want to risk him getting wind and turning up on her doorstep.

Whatever his reaction would be, she wouldn't put Amy's party at risk with it.

It also meant she had one more night to work out exactly how to phrase it.

Picking up her phone, she typed a text to Carrie: *Taken your advice, not going to attend party, will call you tomorrow x*

It wasn't the full truth, but it was enough.

CHAPTER THIRTEEN

HE WAS PACING, A HABIT he had long since forgotten.

Guests were arriving, he could hear them milling about in the hallway of his mother's home, but he'd left the welcoming party to try and reach her once more. She hadn't responded to any of his calls or texts, all of which he had tried hard not to make.

Not even one small text to acknowledge the outfit he'd sent. He knew it had arrived, he'd been informed immediately thanks to Lara's proficiency. So, he'd expected something from her. Even a refusal to accept it. But nothing.

And Amy was late. Which meant all three were late. They should have been here at least half an hour ago. A car had been arranged to collect them from their hair appointment. So, where in the hell were they?

He tried all of their cell phones, again. Still no answer.

What if something had happened? What if they'd been in an accident? He started to look up the number of the driver, a sick sense of foreboding making his fingers trip over themselves in his hurry.

He had the phone to his ear, the call ringing out, when Amy's voice reached him from the hall.

Thank God!

He sped from the room and stopped short. His eyes quickly taking in the lack of Carrie. "Where is she?"

Amy rolled her eyes at him, shrugging off her jacket. "How about a 'hello, dear sister, don't you look gorgeous' first?"

He combed his hand through his hair, his pulse off the chart as he leaned in to give her a distracted peck on the cheek. "Sorry, I just expected Carrie to be with you."

"She didn't tell you?" Now she looked serious, her eyes narrowing on him as she realized his answer. "She texted me this afternoon to say that she was sick and couldn't make it, I figured she would have let you know."

"No." He looked to his phone as if the thing would suddenly speak up and tell him the same. "No, she hasn't said a word."

Why would she not have told him?

"Did she say anything else to you?" he asked looking back at Amy, trying not to react, to not let it hurt…

"Like?" Amy studied him, her features softening as she read him perfectly. "There isn't much else you can say if you are sick." She placed a hand on his arm and added, "She probably just assumed I would let you know."

Why would she do that? Why wouldn't she tell him herself? Surely, he was the first person she should have told? Unable to hold it off, he felt the rejection like a bitter blow, the hurt very real and suffocating.

"Look, if you want to go to her and make sure she is okay, I understand," Amy soothed. "I can play hostess well enough without you…and I do have Lara and mom to help."

Even as she said it, her eyes scanned the people arriving, the drinks reception, and the general hubbub and he could see her jaw tighten. He didn't doubt she would get through it. She was stronger than he'd seen her in a long time. But getting through it wasn't the same as enjoying it. And he really wanted that for her.

Besides, if Carrie hadn't even told him herself then she was even less likely to want him turning up on her. She must have had her reasons. Not that any could make sense to him right now.

"No, absolutely not," he said to her. "I'm staying."

A movement behind Amy caught his attention and for the first time he saw Lara properly. The girl stood awkwardly, fingers tapping over her clutch bag, her eyes roaming anywhere but at them.

If it was nerves that had her on edge, it had nothing to do with her appearance, she looked amazing. In fact, he hardly recognized her. Her bob, normally smooth and sleek, had been treated to a wispy flyaway look. Glasses gone, her dramatic eye makeup made her vibrant green eyes pop, as did the emerald of her satin cami-style dress that, to be fair, looked more like some seductive nightwear than an actual dress.

She looked breathtakingly beautiful, yet young and fragile, and far too attractive to be let out of his sight with the males Amy had invited. The young men had already started to congregate at their arrival and he could read their thoughts like they were his own, many years previous.

Well, not on my watch, was all he could say. There was absolutely no way in Hell he was leaving the party now. Not only was he staying to make sure Amy enjoyed herself, he was going to make sure she didn't enjoy it *too* much.

His role of chaperone to the pair of them well and truly in place, he shot the vultures a warning look before striding over to greet her.

"Lara!" he said, giving her a welcoming smile, his hands coming to rest against her upper arms. "You look a million dollars!"

He planted a kiss on her cheek and felt her still beneath him, but her smile beamed. Perhaps he'd imagined the edge to her reaction. Stepping back, he added jovially, "Please tell me this ensemble didn't cost a million though?"

A little giggle erupted from her. "Of course not," she said, the excited energy coming off her, too extreme to be natural. He swept an uneasy eye over her, trying to work out what she was about, was it nerves that had her buzzing or something else?

"Glad to hear it," he said, trying to shake off his worry, it was probably his mood over Carrie that had him second-guessing Lara's vibe. Positioning himself between the girls, he offered each an arm. "Well, ladies, you are *that* late that I think everyone else is here now, so if you'd do me the honor, I will escort you through."

Lara giggled again and Amy gave him an affectionate tap. "It's a lady's prerogative to be late, you need to learn that important fact if you are going to stand a chance at a happy marriage."

Both he and Lara tensed, although for entirely different reasons he was sure. "I would need to secure myself a fiancée first, squirt!" he said, injecting his voice with a humor he didn't really feel. "Now, shall we?"

They both gave him a smile as they hooked their arms into his: Amy, a knowing look that made clear she was no fool where his feelings for Carrie were concerned; and Lara, one of such adoration it left him feeling on edge once more.

Quickly, he looked away and concentrated on getting them into the main event.

As he predicted, the men flocked to their side as soon as they felt able and after making it clear he was never going to be too far away, he relaxed enough to leave them be.

His mother took the opportunity to bring Charles and his associates to speak with him. The idea they presented wasn't that awful. In fact, he hated to admit it, but he actually rather liked it. He'd like it even more if the chap who was telling him didn't have a habit of spitting with his words the more excited he became. After an hour of it, he headed to the rest room for a reprieve.

What he hadn't expected was a companion following him in.
"Lara?"

She slipped in behind him, her body pressing the door closed.

"Bradley," she purred, her gaze fixed on him, her usual respectful form of address hitting the wayside.

Shit!

He could see it as plain as day now. She was on something, her pupils drowned out the green of her eyes, her skin was flushed and clammy.

"Lara, what have y—"

She pushed off the door and launched herself on him, her hands in his hair as she sought to find his mouth with her own.

"Lara!" He took hold of her shoulders and steadied her yielding body off him.

"I know you want me, baby." She smiled at him, her hands trying to extract his own so that she could come to him once more. "And you can most definitely have me…"

"Lara, please, what are you doing?"

"I'm doing what we both want, you don't have to deny it…not anymore," she said, her body relaxing in his hold as she stopped fighting him, her head dropping demurely to the side as her hands fell to her side.

"You've got the wrong impression."

"Have I?" she asked him confidently, her eyebrows raised.

Christ. She really thought he was into her, it had to be drugs talking, why else would she be doing this?

"You need to tell me what you've been taking, right now, Lara."

She looked to him in surprise. "How I feel has nothing to do with taking something."

She raised her hand to trail a finger down his front and he stepped back on instinct, making her pout. "We're alone now, you don't need to pretend anymore."

She tried to close the distance between them but his outstretched arms held her at bay. "Come on, baby, I saw how you looked at me when I arrived, how you've kept looking at me all night…"

Oh God!

He dropped his hands, horror-struck. He had made her think…it was his watchful gaze that had sent her the message that…his gut twisted with disgust as he failed to finish the thought. He moved away from her, unable to look her in the eye as the humiliation she was about to suffer at his hand tore him apart.

He stopped at the sink, his frame hunching over it as he gripped at the counter edge and tried to find the words. Ones that wouldn't totally crush her and send her running headlong into goodness knows what.

He sensed her come up behind him, and tensed, his eyes flicking to her reflection in the mirror. She smiled at him and slipped her hands over his shoulders. "Hey, relax, it's okay, Amy will get used to the idea of us being together soon enough…"

"Lara, you've got the wrong idea." He held her gaze in the reflection, determined to tell her with not just his words that he did care for her, just not like that. "I'm not into you, not in the way you are thinking, I care for you but—"

She gave him that pout again. "Don't deny it, Bradley, I saw how you looked at those guys out there and how jealous you were of them spending time with us." She pressed a kiss to his shoulder, all the while her eyes watching his. "But you needn't be, they're just boys…whereas you…you're all man."

Her hand slipped possessively down his arm, her eyes following it. "You are everything I want."

The sickening realization that she was far too wrapped up in her own little fantasy to take on board what he was saying had him rounding on her forcefully, his hand grabbing at her wrist to break her contact.

"You have to stop this, Lara," he said, his tone harsh as he tried to get through to her. "You've got it wrong."

She started to laugh, but his eyes cut her dead.

"Bradley?" she frowned up at him, her genuine confusion winding his gut ever tighter.

"I just didn't want them to take advantage of you, Lara," he said, the desperation clear in his tone as the words rushed from him. "You or

Amy. Don't you see, I care about you, as a friend of my sister, as another little sister of my own…no more and no less."

He watched tormented as her eyes welled with pain.

"I'm so sorry, Lara," he said as she failed to speak, his hold and tone softening in his desire to comfort her.

She shook her head. Her eyes darting everywhere but at him. She took a step back and pulled her wrist from him. "I don't understand…you…you," she rambled, raking a shaky hand through her hair, her eyes unseeing. "But you…you…"

"Everything's going to be okay, Lara, we can forget it ev—"

Suddenly, the door flung open and Amy appeared, a look of horror dawning as she took in the scene before her. "Someone want to tell me what the hell is going on?"

Lara spun on her heel and before he could even reach for her, sprang from the room, pushing past Amy and sobbing "sorry" at her as she went.

"What the—" Amy said watching after her, her hand lifting to the doorframe to block Bradley's exit as he made to go after her.

He looked down at her. "I need to go and explain."

She shook her head, her eyes hard. "I'll deal with it."

"I didn't mean to upset her," he said simply, not knowing what else to say.

"I know." She gave him a small smile of sympathy and turned to leave.

"It's not just about me," he hurried out, "I think she may have taken something."

She froze, the pulse working in her jaw, as she looked back at him. "Do you know what?"

He shook his head. "No idea."

"Okay." She started again in the direction Lara had fled and panic welled within him.

"I should come with you."

"That's not going to help," she threw over her shoulder.

"But…"

"Don't worry, just give me some time to bring her round."

He nodded after her. He didn't like it, not one bit, but what choice did he have. Lara sure as hell wouldn't want him anywhere near her. "But if I don't see you again in half an hour, I'm launching a search party."

He was only half joking and Amy would know it. Leaving the two of them alone together when he suspected drugs to have played a part went against every protective bone in his body. But he had to trust Amy enough to let her try.

He watched her race off, his hands shoved helplessly into his pockets as his thoughts turned to Carrie once more. If she had only been here, this never would have happened. And what was really wrong with her that she couldn't bring herself to let *him* know she wasn't coming?

Did he actually mean so little to her?

He shook off the thought. He couldn't believe it, not from everything they had shared recently.

His lousy proposal really had a lot to answer for, but he was fixing that…

Now he just had to be sure things with Lara were fixed first. Relapse or not, he had to be sure she was taken care of.

CHAPTER FOURTEEN

ISLA FLICKED THROUGH THE TELEVISION channels, doing her damnedest to ignore the dress bag that she could still see from her position on the sofa.

She felt like a total fraud. Not just for the obvious. But for letting Amy down and having to lie about being sick.

She took a handful of the popcorn in her lap and stuffed it in. She was an idiot. How she could have let herself feel for a man who wasn't even hers to have feelings for in the first place? They didn't even belong in the same walk of life!

Grabbing her wine glass, she took a glug and pulled her fluffy, pink robe tighter around her. It wasn't even cold in the room. She just wanted the comfort. It was an item of clothing that had travelled with her, much to her mother's amusement.

"You do know it's hot out there, don't you?" she had said, laughing at her.

"Yes, but you never know when you need the cozy comfort…and, besides, they have air con!" had been Isla's honest response. And it turns out the decision had been a rather apt one. She needed its soothing softness right now.

It was pushing eleven, so by her reckoning the party was either coming to a dignified end or turning into a raucous affair. Either way, they'd probably had a fantastic time. They certainly didn't need her there for that.

He really didn't need her there.

She didn't dare think on what his missed calls or texts implied. What would Carrie say if she knew he'd spent the day trying to reach her? Would that change her view on his inability to love?

As if on cue, the vibration that was her phone coming alive against the glass coffee table made her jump and she leaned forward to check the ID.

It was him.

Christ. Would he ever give up?

She settled back against the sofa and shut her eyes tight. As if that would help her ignore it. What she really couldn't ignore though, was the sound of a key turning in the front door behind her.

What the hell!

She just had time to jump off the sofa and turn around before the door opened and his frame filled it, his expression thunderous. He took in the wine, popcorn, and her, assembling the pieces and seeing her for the liar she was.

"This is you sick, is it?" he asked, his voice hard and unrecognizable.

She swallowed, popcorn catching in her throat. "I…I…" she broke off, coughing up the blasted kernel as her cheeks filled with her shame. "I'm sorry."

"Save it, Carrie, right now I don't care!" He yanked at his tie, slackening it off, his fingers working beneath the collar to get it away from his neck. He looked like hell. And still her body responded to him, his raw emotional state mixing with his rugged appearance and making her heart swell with concern while her excited pulse raced.

"What is it?" she said, trying to keep her voice level.

He looked at her, mute, the stress behind his eyes tearing her apart. What could it be that he couldn't just say it? It clearly wasn't about her avoidance of the party if he didn't want her apology. What else could have happened?

Amy!

Her hand flew to her mouth. Please, no. "Has something happened to Amy?"

He thrust a hand through his hair, his eyes flashing. "Amy is okay…at least, I think…or…" He froze, panic rising in his expression and taking her with it. "I really need to get back, please, just come with me, I'll tell you all on the way."

She hesitated, her eyes flicking from him to the doorway, her brain trying to work out the worst that could happen.

"If I told you Amy and Lara are currently locked in Amy's bedroom," he hurried out, "and they won't speak to anyone but you, will you come?"

She felt herself pale. Her mind now at the worst. Not where their relationship was concerned, but the situation the girls were in…

"Please?" he begged, a sheen of sweat breaking across his brow as he looked to her in desperation.

There was no way in hell she could say no to him, the need to make him better driving away any other thought. "Of course," she said, heading straight for the door.

His eyes dropped briefly to her robe and she flustered, shrugging it off as she went. Beneath she wore her trackies-cum-PJs, and right now, she couldn't care less who saw her in them.

"You coming?" she said, brushing past him and heading for the car.

Behind her, she could make out the sound of him locking up, but she didn't wait. Yanking open the passenger door to his SUV, she climbed in and kept her gaze fixed ahead, her mind a dizzying mess of possibilities that had her tummy churning.

"Thank you," he said, getting in alongside her and starting up the engine.

"You don't need to thank me," she said quietly, "I'm just sorry I wasn't there."

He stuck the car in reverse and gave her a momentary glance. She refused to return it, sensing that he was looking for the real reason she hadn't been there tonight.

Before he could ask, she got in there first. "Do you know what may have happened?"

He let go of a breath. "I know what happened," he said, turning his attention once more to the car and putting it in motion. "What I don't know is what's happening in that room right now and whether drugs had something to do with it all."

His hands tightened over the wheel, his knuckles turning white.

She looked to his face, her heart beating painfully in her chest. "Do you think we should call the police?"

"As much as I want to, I don't think either of them would forgive me for it—you are my compromise."

"Me?" she said in surprise. *Why me?*

"Yes, Amy trusts you, when I said I would call the police she begged me not to and asked for you instead." He looked to her on the last and the tenderness she read there took her breath away.

"Why won't they let you in?" she asked.

"Because I'm part of the problem," he admitted, under his breath.

As reluctant as his words were, he was going to have to tell her more than that. Her brain was already spouting all sorts of possibilities and crushing her with every single one. "You want to sum it all up for me, before my mind tries to piece it together and thinks the worst?"

He hesitated, his gaze fixed on the road as his free hand started to rub fiercely at the back of his neck. He was quiet for what felt like an eternity and his distress had her tummy turning. Was she really sure she wanted to hear this…?

"Lara jumped me," he said eventually, his agonized gaze flicking briefly to hers before returning to the road. "She got it in her head that I was into her and threw herself at me."

Isla swallowed, the pain of having her suspicions confirmed setting in. "She thought you were into her?"

He sent her a look. "It wasn't my fault…not entirely."

"Not entirely?"

"Amy had invited some male friends to the party and it was clear they were going to try their luck. Hell, I would have at their age," he added, thrusting his hand through his hair in frustration. "So, I made it clear I was around and if anyone made a play, they would have me to deal with. I was just trying to protect her, not…not keep her for myself, for Christ's sake!"

Isla took on the meaning of his words, her heart reeling as she realized it was his sense of responsibility and affection for the girl he had sought to protect all these years that had sent him headlong into this shit-storm. "So, Lara misunderstood and saw it as you staking your claim over her?"

"Exactly."

They fell silent for a moment and Isla considered the situation she was about to walk into. It hardly seemed likely that the presence of his current girlfriend would help. "The girl is going to be humiliated right now and having me around is like rubbing salt in the wound. Surely it will only make things worse? Especially if she has been taking something." She shuddered over the possibility, she hated recreational drugs with a passion, had seen enough of the damage they caused first-hand in her line of work.

"You should have seen her." He swallowed, his eyes distant. "She was wild, Carrie, totally not with it…I don't know if she's brought stuff with her or…" He looked to her, his eyes pleading. "I just need you, okay?"

"I'm here," she said, her hand coming up to rest upon his arm. "Are you worried she may do something silly?"

His eyes were back on the road but she could see the worry her words had sparked. "God, I hope not, I think Amy would have let me call the police if that was the case. But then Amy…I don't know, what if she takes something too? What if this is a huge setback for them both? How could I have let this happen under my watch?"

His words were laced with guilt, his failure to look after them destroying him.

She looked back on her conversation with her sister, and inwardly mocked it. "He's incapable of love," Carrie had said. What a joke! This man loved with the whole of his being, whether he realized it or not. And she had fallen for him so completely, her lie was crushing her. "I'm so sorry."

"It's not your fault, this has nothing to do with you," he reassured her, unaware of the real reason behind her apology.

"It's not your fault either," she said, the weight of her own guilt making her words smart.

"It is," he argued. "If I'd only realized sooner how she felt, I could have acted differently. But I guess I always knew deep down and didn't want to accept it. I dismissed it as some form of infatuation that would pass as soon as she realized I wasn't all that special and she met people her own age."

"Not all that special?" Isla couldn't help but smile over that.

"Well, I'm hardly easy to love," he ground out, adding quickly, "not that I'm saying she's in love with me!"

"Oh, I think she is, or she certainly believes she is."

He looked at her in surprise.

"I don't know why you're so shocked, there is a lot to love about you, Bradley," she said softly. "Why can't you see that?"

She knew she'd said too much. His gaze softened as he flicked it between her and the road ahead, his hand dropping to her leg as he tried to maintain the meaningful connection that had formed. "So, you going to tell me why you didn't come tonight?"

She looked across at him, her eyes taking in his striking profile, her body filling with a warmth as she finally acknowledged the true extent of her own feelings for him. "I had my reasons, but now isn't the time to go into them."

His eyes flickered with emotion as he tried to read her. "But you will? You'll tell me?"

She nodded. "I promise."

They covered the rest of the short distance to his mother's in silence, each wrapped up in their own thoughts, and she was relieved to see a lack of cars as they pulled up outside. "Have the guests all gone?"

"I asked Marie to get rid of everyone. She's the queen of socializing, she'll have smoothed it over so no one will be any wiser."

"That's good," she said, feeling relieved that she wouldn't have to meet any new faces in her current state, her bluster of not-caring-how-one-looks leaving her as she sat before the grand facade of a house once more.

They got out of the car and headed inside, Isla following nervously in his shadow.

Marie came rushing toward them as soon as they crossed the threshold. "Bradley, thank goodness! She's still refusing to open the door!"

"I've brought, Carrie," he said, tossing his keys on a side table.

"Carrie!" the older woman exclaimed, relief evident in her tone as she stepped around him. "Thank you so much for coming," she said, clasping Isla's hands in her own. She looked every one of her years, the worry etched in her face screaming of her concern.

Despite everything Isla knew of her, all she could feel was an empathy for the mother in distress and she squeezed her hands encouragingly. "It's no problem, Marie, I just hope I can help."

"Please, go on up," she said, nodding swiftly. "Let me know if you need anything sent up."

"We will," Isla told her, releasing her to follow Bradley's already departing form. He was hitting the stairs two at a time, his desire to get to the girls taking over, and Isla followed suit. They headed across the galleried landing and down a corridor with several doors, stopping outside one that bore a stitched heart, the accessory totally out of keeping with the contemporary decor that filled the remainder of the house.

"You ready?" he asked Isla, his face tired and withdrawn now that they were here.

She didn't trust her voice for the pain that welled at the sight of him and she nodded.

He gave her a small smile of gratitude and tapped gently against the door. "Amy...I have Carrie here."

There was the sound of movement and then the door opened marginally. Amy's head poked out, her face streaked with tears.

"Carrie! I'm so glad you've come!" She reached out for Isla's hand and pulled her into the room.

"I'll check on you guys later," Bradley said, looking reluctant as he closed the door on himself.

Isla turned away to scan the room, taking in the typical decor of a teenage bedroom, it couldn't have been changed in years. But there was no Lara. She turned to Amy. "Where is she?"

"She's in the bathroom." Her eyes went to a door in the corner of the room. "She won't open the door."

Moving to the end of the bed, Amy sunk down on it. Her head dropping to her hands. "I knew this was going to happen. I knew she was crazy about him and that at some point she would be forced to accept it wasn't going to happen. I just hadn't banked on a relapse at the same time."

Carrie hunched down in front of her and looked up at her face. "Hey, honey, look at me," she said softly. "This is not your fault and right now you thinking it is isn't going to help her, is it?"

Amy sniffed, wiping the back of her hand across her eyes as she shook her head.

"Do you know if she has anything on her?"

She shook her head again. "I don't even know for sure she's taken something, but Bradley seems to think she has."

"Okay. Do you think she will open the door for me?"

"I don't know, I just knew she wouldn't come out if he was here and there was no one else I could trust. If she has taken something, then mom would only call the police and have her dragged out by force, if necessary."

She hushed her gently. "I'll see what I can do, okay?"

She nodded and Isla straightened, heading for the door. Her mind creating a ticker tape of overdosed bodies, suicides and all manner of other nasties, none of which was helpful to her current situation. Pushing them aside, she tapped on the door.

"Lara, it's me, Carrie."

"Go away, *bitch*!"

Well at least she was alive, that had to be something.

"Look, I know I'm the last person you want to see right now and you won't believe me, but I know what you're going through."

A muffled laugh came through the door. "Yeah, right. The beautiful actress, Carrie Evans, knows what it's like to have the man she loves turn her down."

Isla cringed. She had a point. She knew she needed to be careful what she said, but some of the truth would hurt no one. In fact, it really could help. A plan forming, she prayed the girl would let her in.

"You'd be surprised."

There must have been something in the way she said it that had caught the girl's attention as the handle moved, the door opening enough for Lara to look at her.

The poor girl was a mess, makeup smudged across her cheeks, her hair clinging to her damp face, her big green eyes bloodshot and bright. She knew what people looked like on drugs but right now all she saw was a heartbroken young girl in dire need of comfort.

"Can I come in?" she asked gently.

She moved away from the door, leaving it open to grant her access. Isla sent a smile of encouragement to Amy and stepped inside, closing the door behind her. The modern bathroom housed a toilet, sink, and bath with shower. There were no drugs or similar paraphernalia to see and Lara's clutch bag looked to have been emptied across the floor. There was a lipstick, mirror, mobile, tissues, and keys. No drugs.

Lara sat on the toilet seat, her bare knees pressed together as she hunched forward over her hands, a tissue twiddling between them.

"I know you don't think it right now, but it will get easier."

"What will get easier?" she spat out. "The shame, the broken heart, the pain of knowing the person you care about most in the world thinks you are nothing more than a useless druggy!"

She started to sob, her whole body wracked by the uncontrollable force of it and Isla raced to her, her arms going instinctively around her.

The girl collapsed against her and Isla slid down the wall, taking Lara with her, letting her drop her head into her lap. She just let her cry, her hand stroking her hair as she hushed her gently, rocking her until her body started to calm and her sobs became a snuffle.

"Will it make you feel better if I tell you what happened to me?" Isla said.

"Is it embarrassing?" she blurted.

"Oh, it's plenty embarrassing alright," Isla said on a small chuckle, even as her veins filled with ice at her own memory.

The girl nodded against her and Isla settled against the wall, her head dropping back on the cool tiles as she lost herself to the past and the memories she had carefully tried to keep buried all these years.

"You may not know this, but I have a twin, and hard as you will find it to believe, she was far more successful than me with the guys growing up"—Lara gave a disbelieving snort but Isla continued on—"suffice it to say, she always got the man and I would end up the gooseberry. It wasn't so bad really. I got used to it. But there was this guy we grew up with—Dan…" She told her of her unreciprocated love for him, of how he had fallen for her sister and how devastated she had been at the time.

"That's not humiliating," Lara rebuked, "that's just sad."

"I've not finished," Isla said, shifting uncomfortably as she thought of what was coming next and had to work hard not to bottle it. "You see, then there was this boy Tommy…" Her voice broke off as she quashed the nausea that always accompanied any mention of him, the shame still haunting her.

"Tommy?" Lara asked, clearly piqued.

"He'd been my sister's first serious boyfriend and both Dan and I had had to endure their whirlwind relationship. But it had ended the way all of her relationships did back then. With her telling him she wasn't interested any more, she was bored. And he did what all the others did, came to me for comfort. Normally, they moved on after a short while, when they realized I wasn't interested in a relationship and their bruised egos got over it all, but with Tommy it was different. We became close. He made me feel special, like I wasn't second rate. Plus, he was popular, good-looking, and seemed kind. He came on the scene when I desperately needed the distraction from my own feelings toward Dan. What I hadn't realized, until too late, was that he simply wanted a way of hitting back at my sister."

Isla shifted against the wall again, the memories stinging her eyes as bile stirred in her gut.

"What happened?" Lara asked quietly.

"He took me back to his place one night and totally seduced me. He made sure my sister would turn up while we were at it and made a big show of demonstrating how he took my virginity and it was all her fault."

"Oh my God!" Lara shot up, her green eyes wide. "That's horrific!"

"It was, I was so humiliated, it took me a long time to trust anyone again after that, particularly men." Although Lara wouldn't understand just how long it had taken. As far as she was concerned, Carrie had spent the last few years on the dating scene moving happily from guy to guy. But not Isla. Bradley was the first and only one to break down that barrier.

She shook her head at her, her expression turning to one of guilt, while her crazed eyes darted about. "I can't believe you would tell me all that, after everything I've said and done..."

"Shh, it's okay, I know what it's like and believe me, I'm not going to hold it against you."

Lara stilled and fixed her with a disbelieving stare.

"I mean it," Isla said. "It's water under the bridge and right now you have two people worried sick about you out there."

She snorted at that. "He thinks I'm nothing more than a useless druggy."

"He was just worried."

Another snort. She really did think he thought so little of her.

"He cares for you, Lara." She tried again, "When you did what you did, he just panicked and thought the worst."

"But I haven't touched anything. The only thing I'm guilty of is drinking and...and..." Her cheeks flushed crimson as she fumbled over the words, her eyes dropping to her hands as they twisted in her lap. "And misreading all the signals. How could I have been so stupid?"

"You're not stupid," she assured her.

"But how can I take it all back? How is he ever going to trust me? How can I possibly go into work Monday morning? Christ, he's going to give me the sack!"

The girl was totally losing it again.

Reaching out, Isla pulled her back against her. "Hush, Lara, it really is going to be okay."

"How?" she hiccupped on an emergent sob.

"Believe me, when you walk out of this room and give Amy the chance to take care of you, everything will feel right again."

"You promise?"

"I promise," she soothed. "And as far as Bradley goes, all he wants is for you to be okay, none of what has happened tonight changes that."

She felt Lara take a shaky breath and waited for her body to calm before she spoke again. "Besides, you're the best PA he's ever had, how can he possibly get rid of you?"

"He really said that?"

"Absolutely."

She watched as a small smile crept into the girl's face and, encouraged, Isla rose to her feet, offering Lara her hand as she went. "So, what do you say? You reckon you can put Amy's mind to rest and come and see her?"

Lara looked up at her for a moment, her face one of indecision, but then she nodded, her hand slipping through Isla's as she stood and together they headed for the door.

As soon as the door was open, Amy was across the room and pulling Lara into her arms.

"I am so sorry I ruined your party," Lara cried, her arms going around Amy.

Now it was Amy's turn to hush Lara.

Isla could feel her own tears rising as she stepped around the pair. "I'll leave you girls to talk—"

"Don't go, Carrie!" Lara exclaimed, her hand shooting out to grasp at her elbow.

"But I'll just be in the way," Isla said, her mind now thinking on her talk with Bradley. She needed to speak to him right away, to clear the air and be honest.

Amy turned to smile at her, her face full of gratitude. "Yes, please don't go, Carrie. I would really like it if you stayed."

Isla's head was in a spin, torn by doing right by the girls and right by the man she had defrauded, the man she now knew she loved more than she ever thought possible.

"Please, Carrie," Amy stressed, her pleading voice waylaying Isla's internal debate as she found herself nodding.

"Sure, I'll just let Bradley know you're okay," she said, grateful that her voice remained surprisingly steady. "I'll be right back."

She found Bradley mid-stride down the corridor, clearly pacing. The worry in his gaze as his eyes shot to her squeezed her heart tight. She had to look away; guilt, fear, and a love so fierce rocked her, leaving her unable to meet his eye.

"Please tell me they're okay," he rushed out as he came to stand before her, his hands reaching to caress her upper arms.

"They're fine," she assured him, her voice sounding tired to her own ears.

"They are?"

His disbelief was obvious and she could sense his gaze burning through her bowed head as he tried to read her.

"Honestly—no drugs in sight, just an embarrassed and heartbroken girl in need of a hug." She gave a small shrug on the last and dared to look up at him, her heart in her throat as she did.

"But her eyes, her pupils were so big?"

She shook her head at him. "Have you never heard of pupil dilation when you find someone attractive?"

Does this man really have no idea just how goddamn sexy he is?

"Doesn't explain the nervous energy…"

She gave a small laugh. "I'm not being funny, but if I was in her shoes and had you as my boss, I would be full of nervous energy too."

He smiled then. "Is that so?"

Christ, he's gorgeous. That smile melted her inside and out, and she could feel the atmosphere around them changing rapidly.

"So, for the record, Miss Evans," he said, his tone teasing, "are you also saying you'd be head over heels for me too?"

The direct hit of his words had her heart slamming in her chest. She wanted to blurt it all out, to hell with the consequences and poor timing. But…

"I need to go back in," she said, trying to ignore the flash of disappointment in his gaze. "I said I would stay with them a bit longer."

"Are you being evasive?" he said.

"No, I just know if I don't go back now then I will upset Amy and she's had enough to cope with tonight."

He gave a reluctant nod. "Very well, but you could at least answer that one question."

She considered it a moment and then threw caution to the wind. After all, she had nothing to lose by giving him a taste of the truth.

"Head over heels and crazy in love with you for sure," she whispered, ending her words with a chaste kiss to his cheek.

He looked down at her, his eyes penetrating her own, his mouth parting on some unspoken response as she stepped back. "Go and let your mum know all is well," she said, forcing herself away from his magnetic pull and heading back toward the bedroom. "Come and find me again in an hour or so and we can talk."

The time for honesty had come.

CHAPTER FIFTEEN

SHE WAS GOING TO SAY "yes" to his new proposal. He just knew it.

The expression on her face as she closed the door was so full of love that he'd remained seated long after she had gone. A feeling of contentment, unlike any he had known, filling him as he contemplated a future he'd never realized possible. Not for him.

A life full of love, fun, and…kids?

Would she want children? He thought fatherhood had passed him by, he'd never felt capable of being a decent father figure, not in his line of work with all his travel and long hours. But he controlled so much of what he did now that it didn't have to be that way. And now that he thought about it, he didn't want his work-life balance so tilted in favor of the former anymore. He wanted to spend time with Carrie, making a real life together and if she was willing, a baby too. The very idea of creating a child together had him going soft on the inside, it was just another of the surprising turns to his life that she had kick-started recently.

But he was getting ahead of himself. First, he needed to get the proposal right. He wanted to make sure his last one was well and truly forgotten in her mind. When he thought on the words he had used, the reasons he had given, he visibly flinched. It became more heartless and cold by the day. To replace its memory with the one he had in mind would go a long way to healing their relationship but rather frustratingly, he hadn't been able to reach her father all day. And the man was key to getting it right. In the end, his PA had suggested he send an email, but it was hardly ideal.

It was better than nothing though.

Pulling his cell phone out of his pocket, he pushed himself up off the floor and headed to his old room. He would use the time while he waited on Carrie to help put things in motion. Walking into the old, familiar territory was comforting, it had been his safe haven back then and it was just the same now, only everything seemed smaller, even the size of his acting trophies, shelves filled with movies, and home cinema setup seemed to shrink back with age.

Shrugging off his jacket, he tossed it on the bed and headed to his desk, already launching his email app on the phone and thinking of the words he wanted to say to her father. He wanted to propose ASAP and in an ideal world, he didn't just want her father's permission, he wanted him present when he did it.

He scanned his inbox for Lara's email containing his future farther-in-law's email address and frowned. He had an influx of email, all from Santorini. A quick glimpse and he knew it was urgent, another "emergency" that was being blown out of control. He scanned the lot, the realization dawning that the best option was for him to fly out there and sort the mess out in person. Could he propose before he went, he wondered, the disappointment at not doing it imminently gnawing at him. But then if he wanted her father present, it was going to take a few days at least to sort. And besides, the idea of proposing and then leaving felt just as bad.

No, leaving the proposal for at least a week, made more sense and it improved his chances of making it perfect.

Mind made up, he located Lara's email, and swiftly knocked up a message telling Carrie's father everything he felt the man needed to know and the proposed timescale.

Next, he dialed Chase, the time difference between LA and Santorini working in his favor. He needed to get his arrangements to fly out there underway, but he hated it. He wasn't ready to leave Carrie, but it was just a few days and then he could truly give her his undivided attention.

Chase's tense voice came on the line and they caught up briefly. The easing relief in his employee's tone as the call progressed only serving to support his decision to get out there ASAP.

"Can you ask Anna to sort me the next available flight out of LA? Just tell her I don't mind which flight so long as she can minimize the layover time," he asked.

"Sure thing, boss."

"And tell the team to just keep a lid on things until then."

"Will do."

"Night, Chase." He hung up the call and tossed the phone to the side, his body wanting nothing more than to curl up next to Carrie until he had to leave.

Planting his feet on the ground, he looked to his teenage bed and figured what the hell. He hadn't slept here in an eternity and his mother would probably appreciate them all staying until Lara was safely back home again.

Striding from the room, he headed downstairs and found Marie in the bar nursing what looked to be a whisky.

"Still your go-to nightcap?" he asked, smiling.

She looked up at him, her eyes tired and he would have said she'd been crying if it wasn't his mother he was talking about.

"Can't beat a Macallan before bed," she said gravely.

"It's been a long day," he offered by way of agreement and poured himself the same.

"Hmm," she said, looking into her glass as she swirled the liquid around within it. "It's been a long life."

He studied her, sipping at his own drink and letting the warming liquid soothe him from the inside out. What was she thinking to have come out with such a statement? What was she thinking to look so tormented and drained? Devoid of her high-strung persona, she looked vulnerable and it bugged him.

"That's a bit dramatic, don't you think?" he asked tentatively, eying her over the rim of his glass.

She looked to him and to his horror, welled up, her lower lip trembling uncontrollably.

What the hell!

He couldn't remember the last time he had truly seen the woman cry. The sight was so unexpected and unsettling, he didn't know what to do.

"I am so sorry, Bradley," she whispered.

He took another swig of his drink, his hand wavering slightly and coughed as it caught the back of his throat. "What for?"

"I never meant to bring you up like this...neither of you." A solitary tear ran down her cheek and he followed its path, his eyes unable to meet her own. "I know I can't excuse what happened between your father and I..."

His hand tightened around the whisky glass, his teeth gritting at the reference to his father. He really didn't want to think on those days right now.

"I was young and foolish. I was so wrapped up in wanting to make a success of my life...of our lives...I lost sight of what was important."

"And what was that?" he asked, unable to keep the chill out of his voice.

Apprehensively, he watched her approach him, her hand reaching out for his own.

"You, your sister..." Her tears were falling freely now, her hand trembling over his. "L-love."

He looked at her now. Properly. For the first time in a long while, he searched inside her. Looking for a telltale sign that she was playing him yet again. But there was nothing. Nothing but the pain of a woman that had gone through life alienating herself from those she should have held dear.

"I just got so far down that road I didn't know how to be any other way," she pleaded with him to understand. "But you have to know, I never stopped loving you, neither of you."

She pulled at his hand, needing him to respond. Words failed him. Instead, he pulled her into him and wrapped his arms around her.

"Oh, Bradley," she sobbed into his chest. "If anything happened to you two, I don't know what I would do. I can change, I can. You just need to give me the time and patience, I'll earn your trust...I promise. Whether you can ever love me or..."

She broke off, unable to finish her sentence as the tears overwhelmed her, and he was stunned into silence. He couldn't give her an answer. All he could do was comfort her and in so doing, tell her that he was there for her regardless.

He stayed until she calmed down, making her happy when he said that both he and Carrie would stay the night. He escorted her to her room and headed to Carrie with tired excitement. He just needed to be with her. To have her warm body against his own.

He found her curled up in a ball in Amy's bedroom armchair, fast asleep, her blonde hair falling over her beautiful angelic face, her breathing soft and even.

Amy and Lara were asleep on the bed, both of them in Amy's PJs and looking even younger and more vulnerable than ever. What was it with the women in his life at the moment? He had an overriding need to protect them all. And yet, he was the happiest he had ever been.

Gently, he lifted Carrie into his arms and she flopped into him, not even rousing. He carried her back to his room and laid her on his bed, she turned into it and snuggled down. He didn't take his eyes from her as he stripped off his clothing and climbed in next to her. Pulling her into the curve of his body.

She sighed contentedly. "Bradley," she murmured, her bottom snuggling against his cock. It twitched instinctively and he ordered it to stand down. Tonight was not the night for that.

"Shh, love, go back to sleep."

He closed his eyes, his body and mind content. He couldn't remember the last time he had felt so comfortable, so relaxed, and sleep swiftly consumed him.

She woke to knocking. Her brain totally disorientated as the night's events came flooding back and she remembered where she'd fallen asleep. Only now she was definitely in a bed and she could smell Bradley.

Opening her eyes, she took in a room she'd never seen before. The walls were a mixture of varying blue tones and across one stood a cabinet of trophies. It was a boy's room for sure. But there was no Bradley.

The knocking kicked up again, followed by the sound of Amy's voice. "Carrie, you awake?"

She smiled. "I am now, squirt."

The girl launched into the room. "Finally! I've been knocking forever!"

"You seem in good spirits," Isla said as the girl plonked herself down on the side of the bed next to her.

"I am!" she said. "Lara is like a different person this morning. I don't know what you told her but she is so chilled today, it's like nothing ever happened."

"Where is everyone?" What she really meant was "where's Bradley?" but she didn't want to sound *that* obvious.

"Well, that's the sad thing, he's had to go."

Isla shot up in bed, her tiredness forgotten. "Where?"

"He's had to fly back to Santorini, they're having a bit of a crisis out there and he needs to see to it personally"—she rolled her eyes—"he says he'll try and call as soon as he can and asked us to take care of you in the meantime."

The disappointment was like a lead weight in her belly. Coupled with her realization that she would have to tell him the truth over the phone and she wanted to cry. That wasn't going to work. She couldn't do it without him stood before her. She needed to see him, to read his reaction when she told him the truth. To be able to see if there was any hope they could get past this.

"Hey, don't look so sad! I'll take it as a sign my company isn't good enough for you," Amy teased, play punching her arm.

"Sorry," Isla said, trying to smile. "What about everyone else?"

"Well, get this, mom is in the kitchen with Lara," she said, a buzz of wonder in her tone. "And she's *trying* to make pancakes. Pancakes, can you imagine it?"

Isla shook her head, figuring that was the response Amy was after. "Amazing."

"It really is, I have never, and I mean *never*, seen mom in the kitchen unless it's to get a coffee. She's gone and kicked her housekeeper out for a surprise day off so that she can cook for us."

"Is that why I can smell burning?" Isla asked, the scent of smoke hitting her nose.

"Oh my God, mom!" Amy bounced off the bed giggling and legged it out the door shouting behind her, "I think you may need to come and lend a hand, Carrie!"

She shook off the saddening remnants of disappointment and let Amy's uplifting wake-up call work its magic.

Rising out of bed, she followed after her, her nose leading her straight to the kitchen and the scene of devastation that was Marie's cooking attempt.

"Anyone fancy English pancakes?" she asked into the room, smiling as they all looked to her. "I can definitely do those."

She was rewarded with a resounding cheerful chorus of "Please!"

and nodding heads that had her laughing with genuine joy.

"Let's get to it then," she said, clapping her hands and striding into the room like she owned the place. This could be fun.

Under her direction, they whipped up a feast of pancakes and spent the day doing girl stuff. Despite the odd stab of guilt at her continued deception, Isla had a great time and was grateful for the distraction. So much so, that by the time she let herself into Carrie's that night, it was too late to give her sister a call. Instead, she sent her a text to say she would ring the next day and, seeking out further distraction, curled up in front of the TV, anything to stop her checking her phone repeatedly for news from him.

She found herself still on the sofa when the sun let itself in the next morning. The first thing she did was grab up her phone. He would be there now, surely he would message…

As the phone screen lit up, her heart soared with the illuminated words: *Morning, baby, I have arrived, I will struggle to call today but I'll be thinking of you and will call soon. Love B*

Her excited fingers tripped over themselves as she typed her reply: *I'm glad you are safe, had a lovely day with your family, hope to speak soon, love*—she stopped, she couldn't bring herself to type "Carrie". Deleting "love" she added instead, *I miss you x*

That was no lie.

Carrie had also messaged. *Call me when you wake up, worried about you, Cx*

Lying back on the sofa, she checked the time. It was six thirty which made it two thirty in the afternoon back home. She dialed Carrie's number.

Her sister picked up almost instantly, her worried voice flinging down the line: "Hey, you! How are you?"

"I'm okay," she said, and she really was, far more calm and content than she had been in an age even though she still had to confess all to Bradley. But she was so convinced of his feelings for her that nothing could burst that bubble.

"Do you have your flights sorted?" her sister asked hopeful.

"Now, about that…"

"*Isla*, you are coming home?"

"Not quite," she said.

"What exactly does that mean?"

"It means, I'm not ready to come home just yet," she said truthfully.

"Okay," Carrie said slowly, her apprehension clear. "Why do I get the feeling you have a lot to tell me?"

"I do, Carrie, I really do." She couldn't help the excitement erupting with her response and she spent the next half an hour giving her sister the lowdown on the previous day's events and explaining that she couldn't just walk away. She needed to see it through. She had to try and make it work.

She was expecting Carrie to argue with her, only this time she was prepared for it.

But to her surprise, her sister said, "I totally agree."

"You do?" To say she was gobsmacked was an understatement.

"I'm sorry for what I said yesterday," her sister hurried out. "I've been talking it through with Dan and he made me realize I was projecting my own experience on you."

"You were?" she said in bemusement.

"Totally! And not just that, I have never heard Brad say anything like what he has said to you, in all the time I've known him I wouldn't have thought him capable of saying those things. That has to mean something."

"You think?"

"I do, sis. And if he has fallen for you, then this lie, this deception, it shouldn't get in the way of that."

"Uh-huh." This conversation was utterly surreal.

"You need to make him understand, Isla, blame me for it all, it was my doing anyway, you were just being a loyal sister."

"I was?"

"Absolutely! And don't you take any nonsense from him, let him rant at me."

Whoa, whoa, whoa! This was not what she expected and she felt her mind struggling to catch up with her sister's excited chatter.

"You promise me, you'll stand your ground, Isla, and send the shit my way?"

"The shit your way?" Isla's eyebrows hit the ceiling, it would be funny if it wasn't her happiness on the brink. "I'll try."

"Don't just try, do it! You guys are clearly made for each other."

"God, I hope so, Carrie," she said, her sister's words hitting a nerve. "I can't imagine life without him in it now. I don't know what I'll do if he turns me away."

"If he turns you away, I'll fly out there myself and knock him silly."

Isla laughed her relief at Carrie's absurd threat. It felt so good to be in agreement.

"Make sure he understands it was all my idea, you hear? That *I* made you do this."

"Well, I wouldn't quite go that far."

"Look, it was me that told you to keep up the pretense," her sister insisted. "You told me we should tell him the truth and I begged you not to—remember?"

She remembered alright. "Yes."

"So, there you go! You put the blame at my feet." Before Isla could protest further, her sister asked, "When is he due back?"

"I've no idea, I'm waiting to hear from him again."

"Well, keep me posted, okay?"

"Of course."

"I need to go."

"Why? You have an important date or something?" Isla teased.

There was a delayed pause before her sister spoke, "Dan's waiting for me."

Well, that explained the delay. "Dan again, hey?"

"Don't you start, you sound like mum!"

"I didn't say a word," Isla said, smiling into the phone. Perhaps her sister's turnaround had more to do with Dan than simply a conversation.

"Hmm, bye."

"Bye." Isla ended the call, surprised at how happy she felt and how the mention of Dan hadn't sparked the usual negativity within her.

Over the coming week, Carrie's words of encouragement stayed with her, fuelling her optimism and giving her the determination she needed to make everything work out. Text messages flew back and forth between her and Bradley, filled with promises of what they would do when he returned. She was careful with her responses, wanting to avoid any more lies.

Four days into his trip, she awoke to a voicemail apologizing for calling in the dead of night but he was desperate to hear her voice and to tell her that he would be home by the weekend. She replayed the message again and again. Counting down the days until he would return.

His final text: *Returning Saturday, will pick you up at 7pm, wear the dress! Love B*

Nervous excitement filled her. Saturday would be the night. She had to make it right.

CHAPTER SIXTEEN

IT HAD BEEN THE LONGEST week of his life. And not because of work. That was once again pushing forward smoothly, just as he'd known it would. No, it was because of her. Or the lack of her more accurately. He was going to have to find an effective second-in-command so that he could avoid this dash away in future.

The only thing that had made the week worth it was the fact that he had had the opportunity to plan the perfect proposal thoroughly. It had taken some doing, his spare time being used to make the necessary calls which had left little time for actually catching up with Carrie, but it would be worth it.

The yacht he was currently occupying the deck of was evidence enough of that. He'd called in a favor to secure it, and he had the pianist, the food, the staff, and now the second most important guest—her father—all lined up. And he knew she had the dress. He could remember just how she looked in it. The seductive silver fabric clinging to her body in all the right places, leaving it bare in others…even now, his body reacted to the memory, the force of it made stronger by their time apart.

Maybe he'd been wrong to invite others to join them for the evening, his body certainly wanted her all to himself, but he wanted this proposal to be different. He wanted this one to be about love and family. It felt right to have her father there, as well as his own mother and sister. He wanted them all to bear witness to his proposal and his words as he told her that he loved her.

His only regret was that he hadn't been able to fly her mother and sister out too. He hadn't been able to reach either of them. He planned on flying them both to the UK instead, as soon as they were able. So tonight was as perfect as he could make it. Now all he needed was her.

"Bradley, are you going to join your sister and I for a drink before Carrie arrives?"

He turned to find his mother in the entrance of the sun deck, a glass in hand, her smile warm and welcoming. She was thrilled at the prospect of what was to come, her genuine happiness softening his attitude to her considerably. Things had changed so much since the night of the party. *She* had changed.

"Sure," he said, returning her smile and following her back inside.

The pianist was already playing in the opulent library and the scent of fresh flowers filled the room, calming his sudden surge of nerves.

Taking up a glass of Champagne from the tray being offered to him, he checked his watch, she would be here any minute.

"Has Carrie's father confirmed he can make it?" Amy asked, her voice an excited buzz as she walked up to him.

"Yes, in fact he should already be here." He pulled his phone out to check he'd not missed a call. There was nothing.

"What will you do if he's not here when we set sail?" she asked, a frown creasing her excitement.

"I'll send the helicopter."

She laughed and then stopped. "You're serious?"

"Sure am, he's not missing this."

His mother gave a small chuckle. "Well, all I can say is thank goodness we know she is going to say yes after all this effort."

"I hope so," he said, taking a drink and fighting to keep the nerves at bay.

"I know so. That girl is absolutely besotted with you, my boy," she looked at him with open affection. "And so she should be."

"Lord, mom, you really are turning soft," Amy said, hooking her arm through her mother's in a touching gesture that showed her approval and spoke of their growing closeness.

"Well, it's about time I was," she responded, her hand coming to rest over Amy's entwined arm. "I have a lot to be soft about."

"I haven't even proposed yet and you guys are all doe-eyed! What will you—"

The sound of a car pulling up outside halted his words and they all raced to the window. Sure enough, they had a guest…

"She's here!" Amy gushed as a blonde, silver-clad bombshell, their guest of honor for the evening, stepped from the vehicle.

His heart was in his mouth as he watched her, even from this vantage point he could see her face was filled with charming wonder, her amazement at the yacht clear in her expression. He had done well so far…

"It's polite to actually go and greet your guest, Bradley," his mother gently chastised, her eyes alight with amusement.

"You're right," he said, planting his drink down on a side table and striding for the stairs.

He wished the yacht wasn't so big anymore, three levels he had to descend to get to her and when he did, his feet turned to lead.

As her body stepped onto the gangway, he froze at the end of it, his eyes taking in everything about her. Her blonde hair flowing freely about her, just how he liked it, her dress glimmering in the soft light from the boat and the setting sun. Her eyes sparkling as she stared at him, a slow smile breaking on her face.

"Hey, you," she said, her voice so soft and singing in his ears.

"You need to get yourself across here—pronto," he ordered gruffly. "I think if I have to come there and do what I want to you, we'll both end up in the water."

She beamed at him and did as he asked. Her legs teetering a little in her heels. *What is it with those heels?*

She was a step away and he reached forward, unable to wait any longer. Grasping her by her waist, he swung her body against him. Hugging her tightly, breathing in the fresh, clean scent of her. "I missed you."

"I missed you too," she breathed.

He kissed her then. He didn't care who was looking or where they were. He needed to taste her, to feel close to her, to have her fill his life so completely once more.

She moaned, her body folding willingly into him, and he realized she was heading the same way as him. He needed to break off before he decided to take her downstairs rather than up!

"We should probably head upstairs, we have guests," he said, trying to kill the regret in his tone.

He could see her struggle through the haze of desire to take on board his words. "Guests?"

"I hope you don't mind, I've invited some people to dinner."

"On the boat?" she asked in surprise, her eyes scanning her surroundings.

"Yes, on the *boat*," he said, smiling over her simplistic term for the vessel. "Come, I'll take you to them."

He led her upstairs, the sensation of his phone vibrating in his chest pocket catching his attention. He took it out to check the ID. It was her father.

"I'm just going to leave you with Amy and Marie a second, I need to get this."

She nodded, her attention turning to the other women who were already heading straight to her, their affection clear in their face.

It truly was perfect having them all together. Even if he did have the overriding desire to ravish her.

Leaving the room, the buzz of a message hit and he dialed his voicemail. It was her father saying that he'd been delayed but he would be there within half an hour. It didn't hurt to wait. Perhaps he didn't need the helicopter after all. Which was a shame, he got the impression Amy was quite taken with that dramatic idea.

Stuffing his phone back in his pocket, he returned to the women. They were laughing about some amusing anecdote his mother had been telling and he had the uncomfortable feeling he was at the center of it.

"Are you trying to scare the woman off before I convince her to marry me?"

It was the wrong thing to say. For Carrie, at any rate.

Amy and Marie both beamed at him, but Carrie, positioned as she was in front of them and facing him, went white as a sheet. Gone was the excited glimmer of moments before and in its place, a look that smacked of absolute fear. He'd barely had time to clock it before she was gone, her shaky walk sending her straight outside and onto the deck.

His mother and sister looked to one another in surprise, before looking back to him, the question on their face the same as the one screaming in his mind—*What the hell just happened?*

She didn't stop walking until she reached the bow, grateful for the solitude.

She couldn't remain in the same room as them all, pretending like everything was great when the lie was hanging between them like an enormous elephant.

As soon as he had said the others were in attendance, she had chickened out of her confession. Her brain reasoned that she should at least wait until they were alone again. But the word "marry" had crushed her, its significance making the facade impossible. She couldn't stand there feeling like a fraud any longer, she needed to tell him and the fear of losing him was overwhelming.

Behind her the piano concerto, now muffled behind the closed doors, had taken on a melancholic edge and she could feel the tears threatening to spill. She pressed her hands against her cheeks, her fingers lifting her tears away as she tried to avoid the telltale sign of streaked mascara. It wouldn't do for her to return in that state. Not that she felt anywhere near ready to return. And he was going to follow her, of that she was certain.

She just needed to be ready to face him, to have her words straight in her head, to give their relationship every possible chance of surviving this. But would he even want her when she told him the truth? When he realized how she had deceived him? How she wasn't some talented actress, but a nobody, and an unemployed nobody for that matter?

Nausea hit her hard and she dropped her hands to the safety rail, gripping it so tightly she could feel her nails bite into her palms.

Come on, Isla! she goaded herself. *What's the worst that can happen?*

He will hate you forever and you'll return to England alone and miserable, was her flippant and pessimistic response. But in truth, that was no worse off than she had been before. Just this time, she would be nursing a broken heart.

She willed the confidence of the Isla that had spoken to her sister, the Isla that had played house with his family, the Isla that had pulled his PA back from the brink…but now she was simply Isla, the woman whose heart lay open and vulnerable to the verdict of the man it loved more than life itself.

She felt his approach long before his hand came to rest against her bare back, the delicate touch sending a shiver of anticipation through her spine and a shard of ice through her heart.

"Hey, love, what's got into you?"

His voice was soft and tender, his concern at her disappearance both heart-warming and soul-destroying. The "love" endearment in the place of his usual "babe" was so telling and not lost on her. How could she have let things get this far without telling him the truth? It really was now or never, and never was not possible. She couldn't return to

England and let life go back to normal. She had to take a chance.

Releasing her grip on the safety rail, she turned into him, her head leaning back to meet his gaze, her eyes telling him with every ounce of her being how much he meant to her. He looked dashing and charismatic in his mid-blue dinner suit. His crisp white shirt, undone at the collar, encapsulated his playboy charm perfectly. His scent, clean and masculine, teased at her nose. He was so out of her league, but she had to try, he was *this* close to being hers.

"Hey," she said quietly.

"So, you going to tell me what's going on?" His gaze dropped to her mouth. "Or do I have to work it out of you?"

The proximity of his lips kick-started her pulse and she fought the passion threatening to take hold. She needed to think straight. To catch her breath. She had to get it out quick, before her mind was lost.

"We need to talk," she began, her palm coming up against his chest. She felt his strength flex tantalizingly beneath her touch and swallowed hard—*Focus, Isla!*

His gaze flitted back to her eyes, fear apparent in their crystal blue depths as he pierced her soul, trying to understand her and clearly giving up. "Talk is cheap, I vote for action," he said thickly, his words deceptively confident as his mouth came crushing down on hers, his kiss fierce as he evidently sought to force every other thought out of her mind, showing her with his actions that they had something special.

She was bombarded by the taste and feel of him as he crushed her against him, his hands working to ensure every bit of her folded into his own, possessing her, making her his. The fire he was igniting within her paralleled only with the growing misery that this could all be over in minutes…seconds, if she spoke now. The realization stripped an anguished moan from her throat and she tore her mouth away, unable to cope with the internal conflict any more.

"Bradley, we have to—"

"Carrie?"

She froze as the voice came from behind her, ice settling in her veins as her brain worked to put a face to the man that spoke.

Bradley stilled too, but his expression was jovial.

"Looks like daddy has caught us at it," he whispered in her ear, turning her in his arms to face their new guest and offering out his hand in greeting. "Good to see you, Richard!"

Her dad took his hand and nodded. "You too, Bradley."

"Your daughter and I were just enjoying some quiet time."

Her father's gaze returned to her, his smile affectionate and not at all put out by the scene he had witnessed. "It's been too long, Carrie. I wondered what had kept you so occupied that you'd not been in touch," he said, and then looking to Bradley, added, "but now I know it was a 'who', not a 'what'."

Her voice failed her along with her mind as she looked to the man she hadn't seen in too many years to count. A mixture of emotions underpinned by outright anger ripped through her, sending her dizzy.

Bradley gently nudged her. "Apologies, I think you have me to blame for Carrie's sudden lack of speech."

Her gaze flicked between them and suddenly she was hit with the panic that her father may give her away before she'd even had chance to explain anything to the man she loved. Forcing a smile, she stepped forward and embraced him, giving him a chaste kiss on each cheek.

"It's good to see you again, father."

His eyes narrowed with her words, his smile freezing on his face, the look of recognition dawning. She stepped back, keen to pull away from him, but her blasted heel sunk between the gap in the deck. Nervously, she yanked at it, the move freeing the shoe but sending her tumbling backward.

Bradley saved her from the fall, catching her in his arms, but her eyes were fixed on her father's now stony expression. If looks could kill...

She shook her head gently at him, pleading with him to keep quiet.

"Bradley, it's been a while since I've had the chance to speak to my daughter alone," he said, an unidentifiable edge to his voice. "Would you mind?"

"I'd never stand in the way of some father-daughter bonding," Bradley said in good humor, showing no sign that he thought something was amiss. "I'll see you both inside shortly."

"Of course," she nodded, trying not to sound as terrified as she felt. She was about to get the tongue-lashing of a lifetime, she knew it.

Her father was good enough to wait until the door closed behind Bradley before he spoke. "As amazing as it is to see you"—her father rounded on her, the conflicting emotions clear in his expression—"and I mean it, it really is, you mind telling me what the hell is going on?"

"I'm here for Carrie."

"For Carrie?" He raised his eyebrows. "So, having it away with your sister's partner is something you just turn up and do for her?"

"Father, I know it looks bad—"

"Drop the father, Isla. What's wrong with dad?" He thrust his hand through his hair, his pain evident. "I knew it was you as soon as you called me that. You say it with such contempt."

"Well, that's hardly surprising, is it?" she snapped.

He gave a harsh, derisive laugh. "Well, I tell you what, right now I'm looking like a complete innocent next to you, young lady! What the hell are you playing at pretending you're Carrie?"

Her brain was doing overtime trying to work out what to say, but her anger outrode any sense now.

"Why?" she exclaimed. "Because I'm just not good enough to be her?"

"Christ, Isla!" he said "Don't be so damn self-deprecating! I was referring to the fact that the man you were just...*devouring*...asked me to come here tonight so that he could actually propose to you! Or is it Carrie? I actually have no goddamn idea which!"

"It's me he wants to propose to, we're sure of that."

"We?"

"Carrie and I."

"Oh, well, that's good of you both, shame the guy doing the proposing isn't!"

"*You*, of all people, don't get to judge me, you hear!" she exploded, she couldn't help it, the pent-up anger of her childhood was well and truly on the surface now, her tears coming with it.

His expression broke. "Look, I know I wasn't the best father figure growing up but I tried everything to make you happy. To make you all happy. But nothing I ever did was enough for you and your mum."

She tried to object but the words stuck in her throat. Who was she kidding? He spoke the truth.

"I'd hoped that as you got older you would come to realize it wasn't as simple as black and white."

"You left, how else was I to see it? I was sixteen and you took my sister with you. I had no one left, save for mum, and she was a heartbroken mess."

He closed his eyes against her words and she could see his body tremble, his face tightening.

"It's the truth," she said, refusing to let up. "To be honest, the hardest thing about coming here was the risk of having to see you at some point."

His eyes flung open, unshed tears marring his blue eyes that were a mirror of her own. He suddenly looked every one of his sixty-five years and she felt a pang of guilt. She quickly quashed it. She had nothing to feel guilty for where he was concerned.

"How long have you been here?" he asked gruffly.

"Two weeks,"—he flinched but she ignored it—"in fact, Carrie thought this would be the perfect opportunity for you and I to fix our relationship." She laughed over the last.

"She didn't tell me you were coming."

"No, she wouldn't have, she was in a rush and wanted me to tell you." Now she felt genuine guilt, her sister's rules list had begged her to speak to him and explain what they were doing, where Carrie had gone and when she would be back. "But I couldn't bring myself to do it."

"No, you were too busy making a pass at her boyfriend," her father bit out.

Isla reacted as though slapped. Her stance rigid as she clenched and unclenched her fists at her side. "It wasn't like that."

"No?" Her father studied her for a moment and she watched as the anger left his face, his expression softening.

"No—no—I...I..." she wanted to tell him that she had fallen in love, that she hadn't meant to, but she had. Instead, she crumbled over the words, her tears coming in sobs as her body wracked from head to toe with the release. What had she done?

"Oh, Isla!" Her father was before her in seconds, pulling her into his arms. She went willingly, the years apart forgotten in that moment as she sought the comfort of the man she had once put above all others.

"It'll be okay," he whispered into her hair. "You'll see, we—"

Her father's voice broke off, and his body stiffened. She lifted her head from his chest to look up at his. But his attention was firmly on the door to inside.

Someone was there. And judging by her father's expression, it could only be one person. *No!*

She spun in her father's embrace, her blurred vision settling on the brooding man in the doorway, his expression frozen and unreadable.

"Bradley!" his name was strangled in her throat. What had he heard?

She moved toward him but he raised his hand up, stopping her in his tracks.

"Please, let me explain," she pleaded.

"Don't," he said, his voice eerily calm. Lowering his hand to his side, he shifted his attention to her father. "I came to tell you that dinner was being served, however, if you don't mind, I'd like you both off this yacht."

Without saying a further word, he turned and walked away, the door closing softly behind him.

"Oh my God," she whispered. The words replayed over and over again in her mind as her hands clutched at her mouth. She truly was going to be sick, she was sure of it. Her head began to spin and her vision danced before her eyes. She reached out blindly for support and her father was there, coaxing her to calm down. But she couldn't. Her breathing was coming in rasps now and as the world went black around her, she was aware of one thing—it was definitely over.

"Isla? Isla?" It was her father's voice breaking through into her consciousness.

She came to slowly, the sound and sensation of being in a moving vehicle registering with her. The memory of what had happened, of the dead look in Bradley's gaze as he had looked at her, hit her like a blow to the stomach and she flinched.

The arm across her shoulders tightened protectively. "Hey, baby-girl, it'll be okay."

"Dad?" she said, lifting her head and opening her eyes.

They were in the back of a large, chauffeur-driven car, both herself and her father taking up the rear seat, the lights of LA flickering past and sending the odd stream of light onto the luxurious interior.

"Shh, sweetheart, it's okay, we're on our way to your place, well, Carrie's. It's closer than mine, I hope that's okay."

She nodded against him. Grateful that he didn't want answers immediately. She didn't feel capable of any discussion right that second. In fact, she just wanted to pretend none of it was real.

She let her head drop back into the crook of his arm and nestled against the cushioned seat, willing sleep to come over her.

Sleep meant she didn't need to think. She didn't have to remember. She didn't have to see his expressionless face engraved in her memory bank.

CHAPTER SEVENTEEN

NOT FOR THE FIRST TIME that week, Bradley found himself staring at a pile of papers on his desk and not being able to read a single one.

Four days and his mood was no better. If anything, it was getting worse. As the initial anger and humiliation started to subside, it left a much deeper pain in its wake. One that clouded his every waking moment.

Everything made sense now—the reason for her differing behavior, how she had addressed him, the way she had started to pull at heartstrings he hadn't known existed…Christ, she'd even had his family functioning as an actual unit, for the first time in forever.

No matter what his mind constantly told him she had done, his heart was saying to Hell with it all. He missed her and it was maddening. He was no fool. And the idea that she had taken him for one, cut through him like a knife.

He could hear the phone at Lara's desk ringing incessantly and it was driving him crazy too. He'd figured she'd gone to get his coffee. The drink had been noticeably absent that morning. But she must have been gone at least an hour if the unanswered calls were anything to go by. And he certainly wasn't in the mood to answer them for himself. He'd thrown his own cell phone, still on but silenced, into his drawer to help him avoid callers.

A fresh ring started up, its shrill sound making merry with his already pounding head. He needed to stop the whisky before bed. Or at least limit the amount. But he was finding sleep impossible without it…without her.

Cursing, he got to his feet, wanting to yank the device off the desk.

He strode to Lara's desk. The thing looked unusually bare and her handbag was gone.

Frowning, he lifted the receiver. "Hello?"

"About time!"

"Isla!" His heart pounded in his ears, a surge of unwarranted excitement tearing through him. He had convinced her to stop calling two days ago and hated himself for missing her voice.

There was an awkward sigh down the phone. "It's Carrie, Brad."

He let go of a breath. It seems he was still the fool. "Of course it is."

"Look, I'm sorry to call you at work but you're not answering your mobile and I can't sit back while you ruin your own and my sister's life."

"Me! Ruin my life! That's a bit rich coming from you!"

"Please, Brad, you need to listen to me."

"There's nothing you can say that I need to listen to, Carrie."

He was midway through hanging up the call when her desperate plea reached him. "*Please, Brad.*"

Semi-reluctant, he brought the phone back to his ear, aware that part of him prayed she would say something to make taking Isla back remotely possible. "Spill it, Carrie, and then be gone."

"She loves you, Brad." There was no flourish to the words, just a simple "she loves you". It should have incensed him further, instead his heart swelled defiantly. "And I screwed it all up for her. She would have told you ages ago if I had let her, but I preyed on her loyalty, I used it to stop her..."

He was listening. He didn't want to, but he was, her confession teasing at the lonely ache in his core, coaxing him out.

"Look, Brad, if I'd realized the two of you were made for each other, I never would have told her to lie to you in the first place."

"Made for one another," he scoffed, trying to stay strong. "I'm glad you think so highly of me that you consider a liar my perfect match."

"You don't mean that, Brad." Pain marred her words. "That girl is one of the kindest, most loving human beings I know, and if you buried your pride for long enough, you would realize that too."

His heart tightened. "It's not just pride, Carrie,"—he rammed his hand though his hair, not wanting to add, but letting it come out anyway—"she hurt me."

She exposed my heart and then stamped right on over it, he added inwardly.

"I know she did, but that was because of *me*," she stressed. "Surely, you must realize the reason you are suffering as much as you are is because you love her too?"

She was right. He knew she was.

"You were the man that thought love wasn't for you—don't you remember that?"

He clenched his jaw against the turmoil of emotion raging inside him. "I should have remembered that."

"But she made you realize that wasn't true, she made you capable of love, how can you turn your back on that?"

"Enough, Carrie," he bit out, a lump forming in his throat. "You've caused enough pain, I don't need to listen to this."

"Just give her a chance."

"So she can pull the wool over my eyes again?" he snapped. "I don't think so!"

He slammed down the receiver, his breath coming in quick rasps.

He needed to calm down, to get his head round his emotions and get back in control. He stared at Lara's desk, willing a receptive mood to come over him. Instead, his PA's sudden disappearance bothered him. Where in the hell was she?

He stomped back into his office and yanked open the drawer containing his cell phone. Lighting up the screen, he scanned the notifications that appeared.

Shit!

A message from Lara, one hour previous: *I'm with Amy, we have agreed you don't pay me enough to put up with your crap. Speak to Isla or else get yourself a new PA.*

A message from Amy, straight off the back of Lara's: *And a new sister while you're at it!*

Another message from Amy: *Still love you.*

And another: *Please just talk to her?*

He shoved the phone back in the drawer, slamming it closed. Why did women club together when in a crisis? Surely, he was the injured party in all this?

He paced the room, Carrie's words searing his mind: "she loves you"; "it was all me"; "one of the kindest, most lovable".

Arghh! He shoved his hands through his hair, the pain tearing him apart. Hell, who was he kidding? He couldn't go back to the way he was before, not now that he knew love could be so real and all-consuming…with her. With Isla.

Racing back to the drawer, he yanked it back hard, sending it to the floor with a crash, its contents spilling everywhere. Locating his cell phone in the rubble, he grabbed it up and dialed Carrie before his courage failed him. With her help, he could fix it all…he hoped…

Isla stood before the entrance to her club, her mouth in danger of catching flies.

"So, you like?" came her sister's anxious question from beside her.

Like? *Jesus*, she was taking long enough just to process what she was seeing. It was *her* club, only the funky facelift gave it a new lease of life that had even her itching to get inside. It was similar to Dan's clubs elsewhere in the country, only this one had a feminine vibe that spoke of a slightly different clientele. The exact clientele she had worked hard to attract but hadn't the money to do so properly.

"I know it's different, but Dan knows his stuff, Isla." Her sister sounded really worried now. "I trust him and I know you do too. Please don't be mad. It doesn't have to be charity, you can make me a silent partner if it makes you feel better, but I just couldn't stand back, not when I learned how bad things were. This business is your life, your passion."

My passion?

It had been her passion, it had been her everything. But that was before she had met Bradley. She felt the familiar rush of pain that came with thoughts of him and had to bite her lip to stop the tears from falling.

"Please don't say you hate it," Carrie said, now rounding on her and misreading her reaction.

"How could I hate it?" Isla said, looking to her now for the first time. "It looks amazing."

Carrie visibly relaxed, her face breaking into an excited grin. "Just you wait until you see inside," she said, hooking her arm through Isla's and using it to pull her toward the entrance.

"Oh my!" Isla's eyes widened with awe as she crossed the threshold. Here and there the odd workman still tinkered with an accessory or light fitting, but in the main the place was good to go. It was a reincarnation of the images she had spent years dreaming up, sketching across streams of paper and configuring on mood boards.

"Isn't it fab!" Carrie said. "When Dan showed me the vision you'd been mocking up, since like forever, I just knew we had to make it a reality. The different zones, the quirky features, the lot! It's quite simply brilliant."

It really was, it was everything she'd wanted it to be, her exact vision, only now it wasn't a dream. She wanted to pinch herself just to be sure.

"You're not mad then?"

Isla shook her head, speechless. How could she be? It was the most thoughtful thing anyone had ever done for her.

"So, I can tell Dan he's safe to come out now?"

"Dan's here?"

"Oh, yes, he's just in hiding in case you completely flipped your lid," Carrie laughed.

"Poor guy, he's been nagging at me for years to let him do this."

"And you should have bloody let him! Do you know how much I had to beg him to get involved?"

"I can imagine."

"I had to promise that if you hated it, I was to say he had nothing to do with it, now that you love it, he will of course want to take all the credit."

"Of course I will, it was all my idea after all." The tease came from the man himself as he came out of the shadows to walk toward them, his eyes on Carrie for a long moment before he turned to Isla. "It's good to have you back in the country."

"Hey, you," Isla said, reaching on tiptoes to give him a kiss on the cheek as his hands took hold of her hips. "It's good to see you!"

She stepped back and he looked straight to Carrie. "So, do I get the same greeting from you?"

Isla could read the taunt to his words and glanced from him to Carrie. She was scowling at him, the sparks flying between them practically tangible. But then she smiled, the gesture sickly sweet as she closed the distance between them and slipped her hands over his shoulders. Isla could see his body tense beneath her sister's touch, but his goading gaze remained unperturbed as he watched her raise up on tiptoes to plant an extended kiss against his cheek.

The encounter was over in seconds but the whole thing left a tension in the air that positively crackled.

Revamping her club hadn't been the only thing these two had been up to, she realized with certainty. She felt a bittersweet pang, the role of third wheel making her both envious and uncomfortable. Clapping her hands together with forced excitement, she gushed: "Well, come on then, you two! I want a tour."

Dan reacted first, giving her a grin that told nothing of the exchange between him and Carrie. "Absolutely!"

And off they went, both him and Carrie behaving like a double act as they gave her the lowdown on all they had accomplished while she had been gone. He highlighted the tweaks they had made to her own drawings and why they had done them. She learned that Carrie had pretty much banged Dan's door down when she had discovered the collapse of the club and had insisted he help her fix it all. They had even arranged a launch night that would have coincided with her scheduled return to the UK had she not left early.

But there was no way she could have stayed any longer. Not when Carrie's house held so many painful memories. And although her father had said she could stay with him as long as she liked, three days at his place had been enough. It had been great to get back on good terms together. It had made her realize just how much she had missed him in her life, and it had also helped her understand why her parents' marriage had fallen apart. Although, if she was honest, she felt her parents were still lost without one another. But she was in no place to judge their relationship, not when her own love life was such a mess.

So, after some real daddy-daughter bonding, she had boarded a plane for home, her intention being to focus on the future and what she was going to do with herself. Instead, she had wrapped herself up in the recent past, her mind lost to those special times with Bradley and how complete he had made her feel. She had wallowed in her apartment, refusing to answer her phone, until Carrie had all but broken in to drag her out today.

She could feel the tears welling up again and she forced them back. She would have plenty of opportunity to think on Bradley later, right now wasn't the time for it. She looked to Dan and Carrie, her love for them engulfing her as she thought of all they had done. The two had conspired to give her something so special, something which would have been an unattainable dream just three weeks ago, the least she could do now was show them how happy they had made her. Never mind if it was superficial. It wasn't their fault her dream now centered around a man that hated her.

"I have a dress picked out for you to wear to the launch night," her sister was saying. "It's perfect for you, I figure we can head over to collect it now and I can fill you in on the incredible guest list we have sorted."

"You have remembered that this is Isla's club, Carrie?" Dan's warning tone instantly had Carrie's hackles up and Isla waited for the fireworks to erupt. "Maybe she would like to choose her own outfit for the launch night?"

"I have exceptional taste," she rebuked, "it's what I do."

Dan gave Carrie a look that Isla couldn't read, but her sister clearly got it as she cleared her throat and turned to look at her. "Of course, if you don't like it, Isla," she said, cocking her head demurely to one side, "we have time to sort something else."

What the chuff?

She would have giggled at her sister's remarkable turnaround if she hadn't sensed it would tip Carrie over the edge. The woman already looked like she was brimming with a multitude of rants and working hard to keep it contained beneath her bizarrely-diffident exterior.

"I'm sure it will be perfect, Carrie."

Her sister let go of a gust of air, her eyes flashing triumphantly at Dan. "See!"

Dan shook his head, but his eyes were filled with humor and something else too, something Isla hadn't seen in him for a long time. It was the same look she replayed in Bradley's face over and over again in those moments before everything had gone south.

Panic welled as she realized history was on course to repeat itself, that Dan had been fool enough to risk his heart all over again. Her gaze shot to Carrie, ready to sling daggers, but instead she felt her heart squeeze.

Carrie's smile had softened, her eyes fixed on Dan, her hand toying with the hair at the base of her neck as neither of them spoke, their gazes doing all the work for them.

Isla backed up, her mind working ten to the dozen, a torrent of emotions coursing through her. "I just need to get some air, I'll meet you outside, Carrie."

They both turned to look at her, concern written in their faces.

"Hey, I'm fine, it's just a lot to take on board." She hurried out, not wanting to spoil the moment for them but struggling to bear witness to their developing relationship anymore.

"I'll come with you," Carrie said, moving to follow her.

She raised a hand to stop her. "I'm fine, you guys finish up and find me when you're done."

Dan nodded, reading much in her expression as he took up Carrie's elbow to hold her steady. "Come on, I need to speak to you about one of the guests you mentioned."

Carrie's eyes flicked between her and Dan, her hesitation clear.

"What are you like, sis?" Isla said giving her an easy smile as her genuine sisterly affection shone through, "When will you just do as you're told?"

Carrie rolled her eyes. "Oh, don't you start too!"

Isla gave a giggle and walked off. Behind her, she could hear Dan chuckle and Carrie's attempt at an angry retort was swiftly cut off. She had a pretty good idea as to what had done the silencing, but she didn't dare look. Her heart was too raw.

Pushing open the door to the club, she stepped out onto the street and felt her choked up throat give way, as tears started to streak down her face. She drew curious looks from passers-by and pulled her jacket collar high around her neck, turning to face the building under the pretense of sheltering from the bitter wind.

Christ! Some host she was going to make for the launch night if she couldn't get her head straight before then. It was only two days away and it wouldn't do for her to spend the entire public event looking as forlorn as she felt. It would hardly make a great walking advert for her own club.

Perhaps she could beg Carrie to take on her life for a night. It was a possibility, she'd done it for her, after all…

She really started to contemplate it. The scale of the event was daunting enough without having to do it as an emotional wreck. And Carrie was perfect at that sort of thing, she lived and breathed it. No one would twig…

But asking Carrie hardly seemed fair, not when she had gone through the effort of arranging such a red-carpet affair especially for her and her little old club. No, she owed it to her sister, Dan, and her dream of old, to pull it off.

And if she was entirely honest with herself, she couldn't stomach another switch, not when the last one had ended with such dire consequences.

No, it was her responsibility to do it. Hell, she'd managed some performances lately, what was one more…

CHAPTER EIGHTEEN

"WILL YOU QUIT WITH THE pacing, Brad! It's downright distracting." Carrie scowled at him through the mirror as she perfected her already perfect updo.

"Easy for you to say, I've not laid eyes on her in over a week and from everything you've told me, she looks and feels like hell."

She paused in her preening to give him a hard stare. "Feels like! She could never look it!" Then she smiled, "She looks like me, after all."

He rolled his eyes and took up his pacing once more. The wait was killing him. His plane had touched down four hours previous and Carrie had insisted he wait to see Isla. She had him pitched as the special guest for the launch party and had the whole thing engineered as the ideal fairy-tale ending. For a woman that had rarely given two hoots about being romantic, she was doing a good job of doing so now. He could see the subtle changes in her; an excited spark behind her eye, the healthy glow to her skin, a gentle roundness to her usually hollow cheeks. She looked great.

If he was honest…she looked more like Isla.

"What do you think?" she asked him, turning from the mirror and smoothing down her strapless black number.

He managed a smile. "You look great."

She checked her watch. "Dan should be here any minute."

Her eyes lit up as she said his name, her hands returning to worry over her body and hair. Now it started making sense—the change in her, the worry over her appearance, the occasional deference in her demeanor.

"Will you relax?" he said.

"Says you!"

They shared a smile, one of mutual understanding, neither believing it possible of the other but knowing it was there all the same.

A rap at the door made them both start and she gave him an exuberant smile. "Here goes, you ready?"

"Born ready," he said, striding to the door on her tail.

She pulled it open, her face flushing as she greeted the man on the threshold. "You ready for us?"

"I'm always ready for you," the guy said, pulling her into his arms and planting a full kiss on her mouth.

Carrie folded into him, yielding herself so completely that Brad felt like he was intruding and should back away. But, hell, he had a place to be!

Clearing his throat, he raked a hand through his hair and said, "If you guys don't break this up, I'm going to go and introduce myself, I can't stay up here any longer."

With obvious reluctance, the guy—Dan, he assumed—extracted himself from Carrie's hold and grinned at him. "Sorry, mate, this girl's checking out of my life soon, gotta take it while I still can."

Brad looked to them both wondering just how true that was. They didn't look like a couple going their separate ways any time soon. But then, who was he to judge? He had his own love life to fix. "Hey, I get it, but I'm going to break something if I don't see Isla soon."

Dan gave him a sturdy pat on the back, his eyes suddenly fierce. "It's good Isla has finally found a man worthy of her, that's if you *are* truly worthy of her?"

Geez, the guy looked like he was about to strap him to a chair and run a lie detector test. Either that, or break his fingers under the threat of doing more damage should he ever hurt her. His protection of her was admirable but it was freaking him the fuck out! What was the deal with him and the twins anyway?

"Look, I love her, okay? But if there is some weird thing you have going on with her and Carrie," Bradley said, "then it ends here, Isla's all mine."

Dan gave him a lopsided grin, his arm slipping possessively around Carrie's hips. "That's good to know," he looked to Carrie and back at him, his eyes dancing. "Believe me, this one is enough trouble on her own."

He thought Carrie was going to stamp on his foot, or slap him, but instead she mustered up a smile and spoke through gritted teeth: "Lets go before you say something you can't come back from, Dan."

She started off down the corridor and, chuckling, they followed. They were currently occupying the apartment on the top floor of the building that housed Isla's club. Carrie had managed to secrete him away upstairs via the fire escape, but now that his introduction was imminent she took them through the main stairwell. The odd person stopped and stared, and he could hear the excited whispers they left in their wake.

With a nervous flutter, he realized they were about to have a lot more to whisper about; he only hoped Carrie was right that a fairy-tale ending was nigh.

Isla was dead on her feet.

For two hours she had smiled, talked PR babble and kissed more cheeks than she could count, but the night was finally coming to a close and she could leave knowing it had been a success. Her sister and Dan had really come through for her. They'd fixed the place up, called in the stars, local press, potential clientele, sorted the staff, the catering, the works…it was just incredible.

And then there was her mother and father too. Both turning up to show their support, both behaving like awkward teenagers thrust into a social engagement together after so many years apart, and both wearing their hearts on their sleeves as they doted on their daughters.

She was as happy as she could be without him. That had to be something.

At least the club gave her a distraction, something else to concentrate on, to throw her passion into and divert her thoughts from the painful "what ifs" that kept teasing her of an amazing life, a complete one that had him in it. It wasn't helped by the sight of Carrie and Dan together either, their relationship only serving as a painful reminder of what she had lost, and the cheery facade she had kept in place all evening was starting to spark a monster headache. She could feel it in the knot at the base of her neck and rubbed at it distractedly, scanning the crowd for Carrie. She was more than ready for bed, she just needed to find Carrie and make her excuses first. She'd not seen her for over half an hour. She had left to greet their special guest and failed to return. Perhaps she'd actually bailed with Dan, as come to think of it, he was noticeably absent now too.

"Hey, pumpkin."

"Hey, dad," she said, turning to find him standing behind her.

"Tough night?" he said, gesturing to the kneading hand at her neck.

"Could say that." She gave him a half smile. "A successful one though, that's for sure."

"Something tells me it's about to get all the more so…"

"Eh?" She looked to him in confusion and he grinned, his eyebrows gesturing to a spot behind her.

She spun on her heel just as the music hushed and her sister's voice filled the lull.

She had to be dreaming now. There was her sister, microphone in hand, Dan at her side, and then in their shadow...it couldn't be...it really couldn't...

She was vaguely aware that her sister was speaking, could make out the odd response from the crowd but her vision tunneled, its end filled with a man that looked uncannily like—

"Bradley King," her sister's voice broke through her consciousness, "you want to come up here and tell us all what has you so excited about this new joint?"

My God! It really is him!

On a rush of excitement, she watched him step forward, her disbelieving gaze sweeping him from head to toe and back again. His overlong hair, sporting its messed-up look; his captivating eyes, glinting in the various lights; his tailored back suit, falling perfectly over his frame; his crisp navy-blue shirt, unbuttoned rakishly at the collar. Every bit of him oozing effortless charm. And starved of setting sight on him for two weeks, her eyes devoured him, her mouth turning dry with her parted lips, her body poised as she waited on him to speak.

He scanned the crowd, his face cracking that trademark grin that had the heat pooling in her core and her knees going weak.

"Would you believe I'm actually nervous?" he said into the mic, his eyes flicking briefly to Carrie's as she gave him an open smile of encouragement and the crowd gave a chuckle.

Was this all for Carrie? Was it a favor to her? Did that mean they were forgiven? Both of them? And if they were forgiven, then surely, he had to be there for...for...

She couldn't finish the thought. She didn't want to get her hopes up. She didn't dare believe this could be happening, the risk of another painful rejection keeping her eyes locked on him and the air frozen in her lungs.

"It's not like I don't get up and do these things often," he continued, scanning the crowd. Was he looking for her? She stretched her body out, craning her neck, defying the nerves that told her to hide. "Talking in a public place is simple, but this, this is different. I'm not just here to tell you how great this place is and insist you all give it a try…I am, of course, telling you that too! But I am also here to make a public confession of something I never thought possible."

There were murmurings in the crowd, someone yelled something that she couldn't make out but it had a group howling and his grin growing.

"So, I, Bradley King"—he gave a crowd-pleasing flourish of a bow, and as his head came up, his eyes locked with her own. Her heart kick-started, the air left her lungs, tears welled and her fingers trembled. He held her gaze as he righted himself—"I confess to all of you here, that I am one hundred per cent, head-over-heels, crazy-in-love with the lady behind this business."

The crowd cheered and he carried on: "And if she would do me the honor of getting up on stage with me now, I will introduce you to the true guest of honor tonight, the woman who stole my heart, Isla Evans!"

He gave her a small smile, his eyes dancing in the lights as they stayed with her.

Behind, her father nudged at her. "Get up there, sweetheart. The man has spilled his guts publicly, you can't leave him hanging."

"No…no…I can't."

Oh my God!

Beneath her, her legs started moving, one before the other, their pace increasing until she was positively running, or rather stumbling in her stilettos, the crowd parting miraculously before her until she was stood toe and toe to him. His arms encased her, his face mere millimeters from her own.

"Say you'll be mine, Isla," he whispered to her. "Please say it."

"Always," she whispered back, tears streaming down her face now. "I love you so much."

She read the sheer joy in his face moments before his lips found hers, his kiss searingly deep and sealing her vow to him.

The crowd went wild, and she could hear her sister's squeal of joy. But then she was just a mass of sensation, every bit of her achingly aware of him, and the sounds around them became a distant buzz.

It took a while to register an annoyingly incessant cough and then she felt someone else's hand at her back. "Sorry to be terribly British about this," came Dan's voice, "but you may want to take that upstairs."

Reluctantly, they separated enough to disentangle their lips, but their bodies were another matter, neither of them wanting to lose the comfort of the other.

"I mean, hell, I couldn't care less if you get yourselves off on this stage," he continued, "but the press in attendance may have a field day."

Suddenly aware of camera flashes going off all around them, she felt her cheeks heat. "He has a point," she whispered, looking up at Bradley beneath her lashes.

He gave her a devilish smile and her heart melted anew. "In that case, upstairs looked to be pretty private—you up for it?"

"You're on," she said, slipping her hand in his, and looking to Dan and Carrie, "you guys got this covered?"

They gave her a grin of their own and nodded. To be honest, had they said "no" she would have gone anyway.

The crowd applauded as they made to leave the stage and she gave them all a small smile, the realization that she hadn't said a word dawning on her; he'd introduced her, and then she'd gone all lovestruck and giddy. It wasn't good enough, she could do better than that.

Grabbing the mic as Bradley tried to pass it back to Carrie, she put it to her lips: "Sorry, folks, I've not seen this man in a fortnight and we're long overdue a catch up, but I promise you now, this club will be *the* place to be seen. Hopefully, tonight has given you a taste of that." She gestured around the building, her face lit up in genuine wonder as she took it all in once more and then she looked back to her sister, giving her a smile of heartfelt gratitude. "And now, I'll leave you with my fabulous and gorgeous counterpart, Carrie, and her equally gorgeous guy, Dan. They will ensure your evening ends on a high. Over to you guys!"

She hadn't realized the faux pas of her words until Bradley spoke up behind her on their way out, "Your sister going to be okay about you outing their relationship like that?"

Oops!

Hell, they'd get over it! She was too happy in that moment to let it worry her and, besides, Carrie had to realize now that Dan was destined for her. Much like the guy of her dreams racing eagerly behind her. He was hers. He was truly hers!

About Rachael Stewart

Rachael Stewart writes love stories, from the heartwarmingly romantic to the wildly erotic! Despite a degree in Business Studies and spending many years in the corporate world, the desire to become an author never waned and it's now her fulltime pleasure, a dream come true. A Welsh lass at heart, she now lives in Yorkshire with her husband and three children, and if she's not glued to her laptop, she's wrapped up in them or enjoying the great outdoors seeking out inspiration.

You can reach her via:
Twitter: @rach_b52
Facebook: rachaelstewartauthor
Website: rachaelstewartauthor.com

Also by Rachael Stewart

Unshackled

Dear Reader,

Thank you for reading *The Good Sister*! Many books thrive or perish based on reviews or a lack thereof. Please consider posting an honest review on the site you purchased this book from and/or on Goodreads. If you're new to writing reviews or wouldn't know how to write one, you could start by sharing what you found most enjoyable about this book.

Also, be sure to sign up for the Deep Desires Press newsletter. This is the best way to stay on top of new releases, meet the authors, and take advantage of coupons and deals. Please visit our website at www.deepdesirespress.com and look for the newsletter sign-up box at the bottom of the page.

Thanks again,
Deep Desires Press

WIN FREE BOOKS!

Our email newsletter is the best way to stay on top of all of our new releases, sales, and fantastic giveaways. All you have to do is visit deepdesirespress.com/newsletter and sign up today!

SUBSCRIBE TO OUR PODCAST!

Deep Desires Podcast releases monthly episodes where we talk to your favorite authors—or authors who will soon become your favorite! Find us on Apple Podcasts, Google Play Music, Stitcher, Listen Notes, and our website (deepdesirespress.com/podcast/). Subscribe today!

Support the Deep Desires Podcast on Patreon and you can receive free ebooks every month! Find out more at patreon.com/deepdesirespodcast!

Don't Miss These Great Titles from Deep Desires Press

Unshackled
Rachael Stewart

On a thrilling ride of sexual awakening, love, money, and corruption, 22-year-old Abigail becomes a player in a wildly debauched world where her chance at love might just mean losing everything.

A scorching tale of love, money, corruption, and sex—available in paperback and ebook!

Finding A Keeper
Michelle Geel

When PA Brenna Palmer meets millionaire and sexually unquenchable Gabriel Burke, her search for Mr. Right gets a lot more complicated when he makes her an offer she can't resist.

A scorching hot love story, available in paperback and ebook!

Stealing Beauty
Fairy Tales After Dark #1
Jessica Collins

This time, it's the Beast who's going to attempt to tame the Beauty. The only thing he can't protect her from…is himself.

A modern and sexy re-telling of Beauty and the Beast! Available now in ebook and paperback!

Finders Keepers
Fairy Tales After Dark #2
Jessica Collins

When a sexy-as-sin Dominant shows her a whole new world of whips and restraints, Jayla wants to trust him, but the scars of her abusive past are in the way.

An almost-too-hot retelling of Aladdin! Available now in ebook and paperback!

Incubus Touch
Polar Nights #1
Siryn Sueng

Sex with the dark incubus, Jakai, is far more erotic than Valyn ever imagined it could be. But when Valyn spots a terrifying figure in Jakai's yard, the peace in Tromsø, Norway begins to break apart— and their presence is just the beginning...

A thrilling and erotic paranormal romance—get your ebook copy today!

Wolf's Kiss
Polar Nights #2
Siryn Sueng

Nolan has heard werewolves love bondage and toys in the bedroom, but Halken brings more than just his kinky nature.

The sexy follow-up to *Incubus Touch*—get your ebook copy today!

Body Language
Tim Bartholomew

In this fast-paced tale of beauty and three beasts, an irresistible hero is locked in deadly conflict with a craven older woman out for carnal revenge. Can Andrew's manhood survive in the teeth of her demands?

A comedic, sexy romp in paperback and ebook!

Going Solo
The Complete "Casual Car Sex" Series Bundle
Storm Stone

When a sexy Las Vegas bad boy finds out that his sex experiences with a mysterious Englishwoman are being used for her blog, he decides to extract his revenge, but it becomes a gateway into their deepest, darkest desires, where there is no turning back…

Available now in ebook and paperback!

Heathens
Britt Collins

Murder, drugs, revenge, along with an overbearing family of criminals; JB and Amina will need each other to stay alive.

Available now in ebook and paperback!

Eye of the Beholder
J. Margot Critch
Former professional thief, Isla, is living the straight life. But when her former partner and lover comes back into her life, with a proposition almost too good to refuse, the door to her past comes flying wide open, and it's not just her new career on the line.

A fun and sexy diamond heist—**available now in ebook!**

Power To Love
Power Brothers #1
J. Margot Critch
The Key West vacation Cash Power had planned—a chance to clear his head of the memories of his time as a conflict photographer—takes a turn for the steamyw hen he meets Karen Gallagher, an environmental lawyer who needed a break from her stressful worklife.

Available now in ebook and paperback!

Blue
L.B. La Vigne
A wealthy businessman and rag-tag college student spark up an unlikely romance, but fear of commitment and skeletons from the past threaten their happy ever after.

A sweet (and hot) MM erotic romance—**available now in ebook and paperback!**

Printed in Great Britain
by Amazon